Close call

"Stop, Mr. Olsen!" I cried, nearly choking out the words. "Don't take another step!"

Mr. Olsen immediately froze right where he was. "What is it, Nancy?" he asked hoarsely.

"Look there," I said, "the fifth step down." I wiggled the beam of my flashlight around his shoulder and down the staircase so he would see what I was looking at. "Do you see that?"

He peered carefully downward and then gasped as he saw the thin wire drawn taut across the stairs.

"If you'd come down this a few steps more, you'd have tripped down the stairs," I said.

"I might have broken my neck!" Mr. Olsen declared angrily.

Stepping carefully past him down the stairs, I knelt down to examine the wire more closely.

"Look—it's been fastened to the side of the staircase with thumbtacks," I said. "A booby trap?" Mr. Olsen gasped.

NANCY DREW
girl detective®

Available from Aladdin Paperbacks

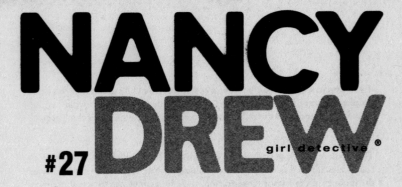

NANCY DREW

girl detective ®

#27

Intruder

CAROLYN KEENE

Aladdin Paperbacks
New York   London   Toronto   Sydney

This book is a work of fiction. Any references to historical events, real people, or real locales are used fictitiously. Other names, characters, places, and incidents are the product of the author's imagination, and any resemblance to actual events or locales or persons, living or dead, is entirely coincidental.

✥ALADDIN PAPERBACKS
An imprint of Simon & Schuster Children's Publishing Division
1230 Avenue of the Americas, New York, NY 10020
Copyright © 2007 by Simon & Schuster, Inc.
All rights reserved, including the right of
reproduction in whole or in part in any form.
NANCY DREW, NANCY DREW: GIRL DETECTIVE, ALADDIN PAPER-
BACKS, and related logo are registered trademarks of Simon & Schuster, Inc.
Manufactured in the United States of America
First Aladdin Paperbacks edition December 2007
10 9 8 7 6 5 4 3 2 1
Library of Congress Control Number 2007921470
ISBN-13: 978-1-4169-3526-1
ISBN-10: 1-4169-3526-6

Contents

Intruder

Trouble Brewing

When Mrs. Fayne called and invited me for lunch, I knew something was up. Oh sure, she'd often asked me to stay and have a sandwich if I was already at the house visiting George, but she'd never *called* before. Besides, I've had years of experience with crime—detecting crime, that is—and my detective radar started humming as soon as I heard George's mother's voice. There was something in her tone. She sounded overly cheerful, but cautious and a little worried, too.

"Is George okay?" I asked anxiously. I put down the file folder I held in my hand. George is one of my best friends. Her cousin Bess is the other. I couldn't stand it if anything bad happened to either one of them.

"George is fine," Mrs. Fayne assured me. "We'll talk when you get here, Nancy. Noon, okay? I don't feel comfortable discussing the matter over the phone."

I blinked with surprise. I'd been scanning my dad's old correspondence files into the computer. Dad's going digital. Saving paper and saving trees. It's a good thing. Besides, I'm happy to help out when I can. I'm proud of my dad too. He's the best lawyer in River Heights, and I'm not just saying that because I'm his daughter. But all thoughts of helping him slipped from my mind.

"Sure, Mrs. Fayne. I'll come for lunch," I said. "I'll be there at noon."

"Thanks, Nancy," she said, sounding relieved.

How weird, I thought, hanging up the phone. I wonder what's going on.

That's when I glanced down at my jeans and turquoise T-shirt. Should I change into something else? Bess is always pointing out that I dress like a slob—only she says it in a really nice way so she doesn't hurt my feelings. I guess I just don't pay much attention to clothes, especially when I've got a mystery on my mind.

I couldn't help wondering if the problem had something to do with the upcoming Jane Austen Tea Party. It seemed that every female in my hometown of River Heights was eagerly looking forward to the fund-raiser, and that included me, Bess, and George. Mrs. Fayne

2

owns a catering business, and she'd been hired to cater the event, which was going to raise money for the local library to spend on some additional computers.

Mrs. Cornelius Mahoney was sponsoring the event. She'd donated the money to build the library in the first place, years ago. She's pretty rich and very nice—which is more than folks say about her dead husband. He was a mean man and probably a crook and a securities manipulator. But that's another story.

Evaline Waters, the retired librarian and a good friend of mine, was on the planning committee. When she asked me to help serve tea and scones for the event, I said, "Why not!" After all, she was the one who introduced me to Jane Austen's novels when I was about fifteen. My favorite is *Pride and Prejudice*, but I like *Emma*, too, and *Sense and Sensibility*.

I've seen all the movies with Bess, who's a *real* Jane Austen fan. She even made me watch an old black-and-white version of *Pride and Prejudice* starring Greer Garson and Sir Laurence Olivier. I liked it, even though the actresses wore all the wrong kind of dresses, as Bess was quick to point out—wrong for the time period. I believed her, of course. There isn't anything Bess doesn't know about clothes.

Ms. Waters convinced Bess and George to volunteer to help out too. But ever since George learned that we'd be wearing old-fashioned long dresses with high waists and puffy sleeves, she'd been trying to back out. She and her mom even had an argument about it last week. Could that be what Mrs. Fayne wanted to talk to me about?

I slipped on a clean white oxford shirt and a blue corduroy skirt. Then I ran a brush through my hair. Finally I scribbled a note for our housekeeper, Hannah Gruen. She was still out running errands, and I didn't want her to worry about me.

Snatching up my keys and purse from the kitchen counter, I made my way out to my car and drove to the Faynes' house. I was surprised to see Mrs. Mahoney's elegant new Cadillac parked out front. Had Mrs. Fayne invited the wealthy widow to lunch too, or had Mrs. Mahoney just dropped in to discuss plans for Saturday's tea?

George opened the front door before I even made it halfway up the sidewalk. She was wearing baggy cargo pants and a bright red camp shirt. She slouched in the doorway, her hands shoved down into the deep pockets of her pants. She was not smiling. This is not good, I thought.

"Hey, George, what's up?" I called out, hurrying toward her.

"Thanks for coming, Nancy," George said, "especially on such short notice. My mom's pretty upset," she added.

"Can you tell me what's going on? Is Mrs. Mahoney here? Did your mom invite her to lunch too?" I asked, shooting one question after another at her. I can't help it. I always ask lots of questions.

When George only nodded, I blurted out, "Then I was right! It *does* have something to do with this weekend's tea party." I followed George into the house. "So tell me what's happened," I demanded.

"Some sneak shattered some expensive teapots, and that's just the latest incident," George told me with a slight frown. "My mom thinks someone is trying to sabotage the fund-raiser."

"Who would do that?" I wanted to know.

"That's what Mom wants you to find out," George said, leading me into the house. "The tea is supposed to be held this Saturday, so you're going to have to work fast on this one, Nancy."

I nodded and followed George inside the house. As I'd guessed when I saw her car out front, Mrs. Mahoney was there—looking elegant, as usual, but very anxious. Ms. Waters was there too. She smiled when she saw me and gave a little sigh of relief. I could tell immediately that she was counting on me to solve the mystery of the shattered teapots. I hoped I wouldn't let her down.

"Nancy, thanks for coming," George's mom said. She hurried forward to give me a hug. Mrs. Fayne's worry showed on her face.

"Sure, Mrs. Fayne," I said, trying to reassure her. "Anything I can do to help, I will."

She nodded and then, turning to the other women, said, "I'm serving lunch in the kitchen. Help yourselves, and then we can discuss the ... er ... the problems we're having with Saturday's fund-raiser and fill Nancy in on what's happened."

"I've said it before, and I'll say it again: I'm firmly against canceling the tea," Mrs. Mahoney declared. She followed George's mother into the kitchen. George and I followed behind Ms. Waters.

"But perhaps we should postpone it, at least," the librarian proposed.

I glanced at George and raised my eyebrows. I'll admit, I was more than a little intrigued. After all, the advertisements were out. What could be so bad that they'd cancel the whole event?

Mrs. Fayne served a delicious lunch—a savory cheese quiche and a fresh spinach salad studded with candied pecans and sliced strawberries. There was also a platter heaped with lots of dainty little sandwiches cut into different shapes, like flowers and hearts and triangles. No one seemed to have much of an appetite, except George, and she's always up for a meal. I was eager to start asking questions, but I waited until Mrs. Fayne had eaten something first.

"These are good, Mom," George said, indicating the tiny smoked salmon sandwiches.

"Indeed they are," Ms. Waters said. "I hope you'll be serving them on Saturday." Then, with an uncertain clearing of her throat, she added, "*If* there's still going to be a tea on Saturday."

There was an immediate protest from both Mrs. Fayne and Mrs. Mahoney, and I used this as my opening to jump in and start asking questions.

"So, tell me what's going on," I urged. "George mentioned something about sabotage. Are you really considering canceling the Jane Austen Tea Party?"

"We may have to," Ms. Waters said quietly.

"We *can't*," Mrs. Fayne protested. "Not after all our hard work and publicity efforts," she added, refilling our glasses with iced tea.

"I agree," Mrs. Mahoney spoke up. "Ticket sales have been better than we'd expected, and I have no doubt we'll sell many last-minute ones at the door. The tea must go on as scheduled."

"Not if there's the possibility that someone may get hurt," Ms. Waters insisted.

"Mrs. Fayne, please start at the beginning," I urged.

George's mom looked at me with a worried frown. "Nancy, as you know, the fund-raiser is supposed to be held at Cardinal Corners, the new bed-and-breakfast owned by Mr. and Mrs. Olsen."

7

I nodded. I'd driven past the big old house with its sprawling lawns more than a week ago. The locals referred to it as "the old Rappapport place." It dated all the way back to Civil War days and was located not far from the river. It had been pretty run-down until Mr. and Mrs. Olsen arrived from Iowa and started fixing it up. The bed-and-breakfast was supposed to open for business right after the fund-raiser was over.

"Mrs. Olsen says she's heard strange noises in the night," George's mom went on. "Furniture has been rearranged and even tipped over. Once, the beds were stripped of all the sheets and blankets and left in a heap in the middle of the upstairs hall."

"And now, the unexplained teapot incident," Ms. Waters said with a sigh.

"What teapot incident?" I asked. I needed to know all the specifics if I was going to successfully get to the bottom of the mystery.

"Most of the teapots we've borrowed for Saturday's event," Mrs. Mahoney said, "were from Evaline's collection." She shot a sympathetic glance at Ms. Waters. "They were broken to bits, and two of the valuable silver ones have been seriously damaged."

"Did this take place at the Olsens'?" I asked. When all the women nodded, I went on. "Were there any signs of breaking and entering? Did they call the police?"

"Not at first," Mrs. Fayne said. "Nothing was stolen or damaged until the teapots. But Carol Olsen did call Chief McGinnis first thing this morning. He said it was probably vandals, but without witnesses the chances of catching them are slim."

I nodded. I could imagine how Mrs. Olsen's worried phone call was received at headquarters. Chief McGinnis is not one of my favorite people. But I have to admit, he's a good law enforcement officer and has helped me with several cases in the past. Of course, Bess and George are usually quick to point out that I've helped him more than he's ever helped me.

"So, any ideas who could have done it?" I asked. "Were there any fingerprints?"

The women shook their heads.

"What about footprints outside the house, around the windows and doors?" I went on.

Again, the women shook their heads and shrugged.

"I'm afraid someone is deliberately trying to prevent the tea party from taking place," Mrs. Fayne said.

"And something worse could happen between now and Saturday. Someone could be hurt. What if there's a serious accident?" Ms. Waters asked. She looked so nervous that I wondered briefly if she knew something she wasn't telling the rest of us.

Mrs. Mahoney gave an indignant snort. "Why would anyone want to sabotage the event?" she demanded. "After all, it's a community benefit. The public library will get new computers that everyone can use."

"Mom, tell Nancy what Mrs. Olsen told you," George said. Mrs. Fayne looked sort of uncomfortable and became suddenly busy folding the corner of her napkin over and over again. I looked at George expectantly.

"I need to know everything," I prompted. "There's not much time. It's already Tuesday and the Jane Austen Tea Party is planned for Saturday afternoon."

Mrs. Fayne hesitated. She glanced uncomfortably at Mrs. Mahoney. Mrs. Mahoney in turn looked over at Evaline Waters. Finally George blurted, "Mrs. Olsen thinks her house is haunted by a mean ghost!"

A Tempest and Some Teapots

A **ghost?" I declared.** "She thinks the house is haunted?"

George nodded and gave an embarrassed little shrug. Mrs. Mahoney snorted with disapproval.

"But there's never been any ghost stories associated with the old Rappapport place," Ms. Waters added thoughtfully. "At least none that I can remember."

"It's all nonsense," Mrs. Fayne put in. "We can't cancel a much-anticipated fund-raiser because of a silly ghost story. Besides, I don't think Carol really believes there's a ghost. It's the cleaning woman who's convinced the house is haunted."

"Emily Spradling is frightened of her own shadow," Mrs. Mahoney put in.

"Who is Emily Spradling?" I asked, grinning. She

sounded like a real goose. I wondered if the Olsens had mentioned this little angle to Chief McGinnis. I could just imagine his reaction to their suggestion of a ghostly vandal rather than a human one.

"Emily is the one who has seen the ghost that is supposedly shattering teapots and messing up the bed linens. She works for the Olsens," Mrs. Mahoney explained. "Won't you go out to the bed-and-breakfast and investigate, Nancy? We'd all feel so much better if you'd look into the matter for us."

"Yes, Nancy, please," Mrs. Fayne urged. "We must go on with the fund-raiser."

"But we don't want any more mishaps between now and then," Ms. Waters said, leaning toward me. "You'll solve the mystery, won't you?"

"I'll certainly try," I said. "If you'll let George come along, I'd like to go out there now, Mrs. Fayne. Will you call the Olsens and let them know we're coming?"

The three women seemed quite relieved by my take-charge attitude. Reassured, Mrs. Mahoney and Ms. Waters finished their lunch, then thanked our hostess and left together a short while later. George and I cleared the table while Mrs. Fayne called the Olsens. I was wondering who was reading the paperback copy of Jane Austen's novel *Emma* that I noticed on the kitchen counter when George spoke up.

"So, what do you think, Nancy?" she probed. "Any chance there's a real ghost at Cardinal Corners?"

When I saw the smile that was tugging at the corner of my friend's mouth, I chuckled. "I'm not scared. Are you?"

George grinned. "Not in broad daylight, anyway," she said.

But by the time we'd finished helping Mrs. Fayne in the kitchen, the sky had grown dark with rain clouds. As George and I drove out to Cardinal Corners, the weather became even more threatening. We'd only been on the road for fifteen minutes when the heavy clouds opened up and drops poured down. I turned on my windshield wipers, but I could still barely see through the streaming rain.

"I think I'd better slow down," I said. The wipers were flapping like crazy. "I can't see a thing. George, you'll have to help me look for the turnoff."

George peered through the windows. Just then a clap of thunder boomed overhead and a jagged flash of lightning illuminated the highway. We both jumped.

"Just what we need—a thunderstorm on our way to a haunted house." George laughed uneasily.

I only nodded, too preoccupied with driving cautiously to carry the joke any further. "There it is!" George declared. "I just saw the sign with the red bird on it—that must be Cardinal Corners up ahead."

We soon saw the old three-story house rise up through the gloom. The lights were on, giving a welcoming glow in the dark, stormy afternoon.

"That must be Mrs. Olsen," I said, pulling my car into the driveway as near to the veranda steps as possible. A short, red-haired woman with a blue sweater slung around her shoulders stood near the front door.

"We'll have to make a dash for it," George said. "And watch out for puddles."

"Okay, here goes," I replied, tucking my car keys into my purse. George and I ran like crazy up the steps of the B and B. We were wet, breathless, and laughing when the red-haired woman opened the front door for us.

"Come in, girls, before you drown," she urged. "Thank goodness you've arrived safely. You must be Nancy Drew?" she said, looking up at me anxiously.

"Yes, ma'am," I replied, shaking the rain from my skirt and swiping a hand through my damp hair. Up close, the woman looked much older. Her face was lined with wrinkles, and her curly red hair was heavily streaked with gray. But her brown eyes were vibrant and so was her smile.

"You must be Mrs. Olsen," I said as we shook hands. Mine was slightly damp. "This is my friend George Fayne."

"I've met your mother, George," Mrs. Olsen said,

shaking my friend's hand, too. "Come in and dry off. I've got hot water on. We'll have some tea—or coffee, if you'd prefer it."

I opted for hot tea. George wanted coffee. We dried off a little in the bathroom down the hall and then made our way back to the foyer, where we rejoined Mrs. Olsen. She then led us to an old-fashioned parlor with a warm fire crackling in the fireplace. A tall, skinny man had assembled cups and saucers and platters of cookies.

"This is my husband, Karl," Mrs. Olsen said. George and I shook hands with Mr. Olsen. He was so thin that his Adam's apple bobbed up and down his throat when he spoke.

"You've restored this old house beautifully," I told the couple. They seemed pleased by the compliment, and Mr. Olsen indicated some of the work they'd done to the tall, arched windows and high ceilings. Glancing around, I smiled slightly when I noticed the copy of *Northanger Abbey* by Jane Austen on the end table near Mrs. Olsen's chair. That was one of Jane Austen's novels I hadn't read yet, but I hoped to get around to it one of these days.

As we sipped our hot drinks, Mrs. Olsen explained that she and her husband were both retired schoolteachers, and that they'd always dreamed of owning a bed-and-breakfast one day. They'd discovered the old

Rappapport place while on a road trip more than a year ago and had fallen in love with it.

"Our first official day of business will be Saturday, when we host the Jane Austen Tea Party," Mr. Olsen told us as he passed the cookies. "We already have customers booked for that weekend, and now, with the recent vandalism, we're a little nervous to accept any more reservations."

"Our life savings are tied up in this enterprise. We can't quit, no matter what terrible things happen. We have no place else to go," Mrs. Olsen said, wringing her hands. "No one ever mentioned the possibility that the house might be . . . well, you know . . . haunted," she added nervously.

"I told Carol that a good old-fashioned ghost might be good for business," Mr. Olsen said with a throaty chuckle.

"I'm not interested in *that* sort of business," Mrs. Olsen replied curtly. "Can you help us, Nancy? Mrs. Fayne and the other women on the planning committee told us that you could."

"Nancy does have a real knack for solving mysteries," George spoke up.

Compliments always embarrass me a little. "I'll certainly give it my best shot," I assured them. "First tell me all that's happened. Have either of you actually seen the ghost?"

"Emily claims she's heard the ghost on more than one occasion," Mrs. Olsen said with a sniff. "Emily works for us. Helps out in the kitchen and does the laundry, makes the beds. Frankly I don't think it's a ghost. I think someone is trying to run us out of business before we even get started."

"Why?" I asked.

"Maybe they don't want the competition," Mr. Olsen ventured. "There *are* other B and Bs in town."

"You told Chief McGinnis about the vandalism, right?" I pressed.

"We told him about the broken teapots," Mr. Olsen admitted. "But the other incidents have been . . . well . . . *strange*."

"You mean the tipped-over furniture and rumpled bed linens?" I asked.

The Olsens nodded.

"Once, we were jolted out of a sound sleep by a lot of banging coming from the kitchen," Mrs. Olsen said. "When we came downstairs, we didn't find anybody. But all the kitchen cabinets were flung open. Pots and pans and casserole dishes were scattered all over the floor."

"Furniture has been moved once or twice, and all the mirrors hung crooked," her husband added.

"But nothing broken or destroyed?" George asked.

"Not until the teapots yesterday," Mr. Olsen said.

"I feel just awful about that too," Mrs. Olsen added. "Most of the broken ones belonged to Evaline Waters."

"Did you tell anybody else, other than the women on the fund-raiser committee, about what's happened?" I asked.

Mr. Olsen chuckled dryly. "A fine pair of goonies we'd seem to be if we called the police about these sorts of incidents. And since we're new to the community, we don't know who to trust. We're a little afraid, really, to talk about what's been happening, and we don't want any negative publicity."

"Strange things just keep happening," Mrs. Olsen admitted. "I'll confess I'm very worried."

So was I, but I didn't say anything. I glanced at one of the tall arched windows and watched the rain pouring outside. There was a boom of thunder in the distance, and I made up my mind to get to work immediately. The random acts of vandalism or ghostly mischief were becoming increasingly destructive. Still, I didn't think Chief McGinnis would give the crime a high priority. It would be up to me to solve the case.

"The police dusted for prints," Mr. Olsen said then. I looked up from my teacup. "They had a look around but didn't find anything," he added with a shrug.

"And we only called because of the broken teapots," Mrs. Olsen added. "We didn't tell them about . . . about the *other* things that happened."

"We didn't want them to think we were kooks or anything," her husband said.

"Nancy, do you think a ghost is haunting Cardinal Corners?" Mrs. Olsen looked at me uncertainly.

"No," I replied. "I think someone wants to scare you. Who and why I don't know, but I intend to find out."

"What about the teapots?" George asked me. "You don't think they were destroyed to prevent the tea party from taking place?"

"No, I think they were broken because they were easy and convenient items to break," I said.

"So, it was not meant to sabotage the fund-raiser?" Mr. Olsen asked.

"I'm not sure," I told him. "It's just a hunch, but I don't think these incidents have anything to do with the fund-raiser. The pranks are rather childish. If someone wanted to sabotage Saturday's tea, why not break into the Faynes' home and destroy the centerpieces and baked goods Mrs. Fayne has stored there?"

There was a brief silence after I posed this question. No one said a word. The only sound was the steady downpour of rain outside and the occasional rumble of thunder. I really wanted to have a look around the old place and see if anybody was getting inside through a back door or window somewhere. But the weather wasn't cooperating.

"Does anyone live here with you?" I asked, deciding to pursue another angle. "Any employees?"

"We have only two people working for us so far," Mrs. Olsen said, again passing me the plate of cookies. "I've already told you about Emily."

"She's a timid little thing," Mr. Olsen said. "Emily's quite convinced that a ghost is responsible for all that's been happening. She told us that she's heard it more than once and insists that she saw it too in the hallway upstairs. She seems sincerely frightened."

"Juan Tabo comes several times a week to do the yard work," Mrs. Olsen went on. "He's a rather surly young man, but he keeps the grounds looking quite lovely, and his garden shed is neat and tidy. He's very reliable, too, and always shows up on time, rain or shine."

"I'd like to speak with both of them," I told the Olsens. "And I'd like to have a look around the place. Obviously I'm not going to be able to search the grounds for clues this afternoon. I'll start inside the house." I rose to my feet. There was no time to waste.

"Do you keep any valuables here?"

"No, just the usual sort of things—the televisions, a camera, the computer," Mr. Olsen said, hauling his lanky frame from his chair.

"My mother's silverware," Mrs. Olsen put in. "When you look around, what are you expecting to find?"

"I'm not *expecting* to find anything in particular," I said, placing my empty cup and saucer on a small side table.

"Nancy wants to look for clues," George explained.

"There's also the possibility that one of your employees is responsible for these pranks," I said, looking at the couple. They both frowned when I mentioned this.

"I really don't think—" Mrs. Olsen's statement ended abruptly and with a gasp as the lights blinked out, plunging the entire house in sudden darkness. Before anyone could say a word, the silence was pierced by a woman's terrified scream!

3

Deadly Danger

"Who was that?" I demanded, stooping down for my purse. I quickly retrieved my car keys, which had a tiny flashlight attached to the key ring. This little tool had come in pretty handy on several occasions. I flicked it on and stood up. "Where did that scream come from?" I asked.

"I think it was Emily," Mrs. Olsen stammered. "She's in the kitchen."

"Lead the way to the kitchen, Mr. Olsen," I urged, "and hurry!"

The scream had been awful. I feared the worst. I glanced at George, and even in the gloom I could see the tension on her face. She was worried too.

My heart was pounding as I hurried along behind Mr. Olsen. George and Mrs. Olsen followed me.

When we all reached the kitchen, Emily Spradling was alive and well, standing on her own two feet. The gleam of my flashlight revealed her to be a middle-aged woman in a dark dress and an apron. Her brown hair was pulled back in a limp ponytail. She clutched her chest with one hand and clung to the kitchen counter with the other.

"Emily, are you all right?" Mrs. Olsen asked, rushing forward to steady her frightened employee.

"The ghost. It was . . . *there!*" She pointed to what looked like a small broom closet. While Mr. Olsen rummaged through the kitchen cabinets retrieving chunky pillar candles and matches, I yanked open the door to the little closet.

"It's a dumbwaiter!" I declared. I stepped aside so George could have a look at the small elevator that was used in the old days to send food to the rooms upstairs. I'd seen these contraptions in old houses before, and I poked my head in, wondering if it would bear my weight.

George hissed in my ear, "Don't even think about getting in there, Nancy Drew."

I shrugged. "You saw the ghost in here?" I asked, turning to Emily.

The woman, wide-eyed with fear, nodded. "I saw the dumbwaiter move—right before the lights went out."

23

"But you didn't actually see the ghost," I pressed.

"I heard it—in there," Emily insisted, pointing to the dumbwaiter.

I frowned and turned back to examine the dumb-waiter.

George whispered, "If anything happens to you, you could end up in the hospital—or worse. Then who would solve this case before Saturday?" she asked.

I reluctantly gave up the idea of cramming myself into the dumbwaiter and going from floor to floor looking for the intruder. George was right. I had to be careful. A lot of people were depending on me.

"It *is* large enough for a person to get into," I said. "A young teenager or even a small man or woman could get from floor to floor in here."

"It was a ghost," Emily insisted with a shudder. Then she started to cry. As Mrs. Olsen talked to her in soothing tones and helped her to a chair at the kitchen table, I glanced at George, who wrinkled her nose slightly. She was thinking the same thing I was: Emily was not a good witness.

"Mr. Olsen, is the electricity off in the entire neighborhood or just here in your house?" I asked, steering the conversation in a different direction.

Mr. Olsen, who'd finished lighting candles, replied, "There's one quick way to find out." Picking up the large flashlight he'd found in a kitchen drawer, he made his way to the dining room and peered out the window. I stood in the doorway watching him and turned off my own miniflashlight.

"The streetlamp is on, and I can see lights from the Williams' house down the road," he called out. "Looks like this place is the only one without electricity."

"Okay," I said, "then we'd better take a look at your fuse box."

"Do you want to call the police?" George asked, turning to me first and then the Olsens.

Just then the back door of the kitchen opened. A young Hispanic man wearing jeans and a red windbreaker stepped in through the door. He was soaking wet and slightly breathless, as though he'd been running. He wiped his muddy boots on the mat and removed his St. Louis Cardinals ball cap. "Mr. Olsen, I can't work in this downpour," he complained. "I'll come back tomorrow."

"This is the gardener, Juan Tabo," Mr. Olsen said, turning to me.

When Mr. Olsen introduced George and me, Juan scowled slightly. Looking at me, he said, "You're the girl detective. I've read about you in the newspapers."

"Nice watch," I said, glancing at his left wrist. "Hope it didn't get wet."

Without taking his eyes off my face, Juan jerked the sleeves of his jacket down over his wrists. "I'll see

25

you tomorrow then," he said, turning to Mr. Olsen. Before I could ask him if he'd seen anybody on the grounds, he was out the door and gone.

"Friendly fellow," George said sarcastically.

"Don't you think it's odd that he didn't even comment on the fact that we're sitting here in the kitchen with the candles lit and no electricity?" I asked. George nodded.

"Do you want me to call the police or not?" she asked again.

Mrs. and Mr. Olsen looked at each other and shook their heads. "And tell them what? That Emily thought she heard a ghost in the dumbwaiter?" Mr. Olsen asked.

"It *was* a ghost!" Emily insisted with a watery sniff.

"I think someone is or was in your house. He or she could still be hiding here somewhere. Exactly where does the dumbwaiter go?" I asked.

"Down to the basement and all the way up to the third floor," Mrs. Olsen replied. "It will come in handy when we have paying guests who want breakfast in bed."

"I want to look around," I said. "George, take a look at the fuse box, would you? And call Hannah— tell her I'll be late for dinner."

"Sure thing, Nancy," George said. "I'd better call my mom, too."

26

"If you want to go upstairs to look around, I'll come with you," Mr. Olsen volunteered. "Carol, you can show George the fuse box."

"I want to go home," Emily whined. "My husband won't like it, me working here . . . with ghosts and all."

"You don't want to drive home in this downpour, do you?" Mrs. Olsen said. "As soon as the rain lets up some, you can go home early. I wish I could make you a good strong cup of hot tea," she lamented. "But without electricity, there's no way to heat the water."

"Juan went home, and I'm going home too," Emily insisted. She shoved the chair away from the table, stood up, and quickly retrieved her purse from the utility room off the kitchen. Giving a sniff, she left the house through the back door, holding an umbrella over her head.

"We'll be back shortly," I said to George and Mrs. Olsen. I was eager to see if someone might still be in the house. I could question Emily another time, when she was calmer. Turning to Mr. Olsen, I flicked my miniflashlight on again and said, "Lead the way."

We went upstairs, checking out both the second and third floors. I kept wondering how the intruder got into the house without being seen. I figured he had access to every floor using the dumbwaiter.

"This guy is pretty bold, breaking in during the daytime like this," Mr. Olsen said.

"Yes," I agreed. "He's either very foolish or very desperate. With this storm raging, he must have known everyone would be in the house. That increases his chances of being seen or even caught."

On the second and third floors, Mr. Olsen showed me where the dumbwaiter was located. I looked around for evidence of muddy footprints, but I didn't find anything.

"So, the prowler had been in the house long before the storm started, and that's why he didn't leave any muddy footprints," I said, thinking out loud. But did the trespasser intentionally or unintentionally scare Emily? I wondered.

I poked my head into all the empty bedrooms upstairs and thought what a perfect place this would be to spend a leisurely weekend—with breakfast in bed. It was also the perfect place for a sneaky intruder to play hide-and-seek.

"Where does this staircase go?" I asked. I aimed my flashlight down another flight of stairs at the opposite end of the corridor.

"These are the back stairs," Mr. Olsen explained. "It's a shortcut to the kitchen. You don't go through the entrance hall and parlor this way."

"We might as well rejoin the others," I said with a short sigh. "There's just so much I can see and do without lights."

"Can you come back tomorrow, Nancy?" Mr. Olsen asked. "I'm hoping the sun will be out, and you can look around all you want. You can check out the basement and the grounds then too," he added. "Let's go down this way."

He pointed the bright beam of his large flashlight at the steps before us and took a step down. Aiming my smaller beam at his feet and ankles, I started down the stairs behind him. Suddenly I caught the gleam of something on the stairs in front of Mr. Olsen. My heart skipped a beat, and I grabbed him by the sleeve of his sweater.

"Stop, Mr. Olsen!" I cried, nearly choking out the words. "Don't take another step!"

4

Scones and Schemes

Mr. Olsen immediately froze right where he was. "What is it, Nancy?" he asked hoarsely.

"Look there," I said. "The fifth step down." I wiggled the beam of my flashlight around his shoulder and down the staircase so he would see what I was looking at. "Do you see that?"

He peered carefully downward and then gasped as he saw the thin wire drawn taut across the stairs.

"If you'd come down a few steps more, you'd have tripped down the stairs," I said.

"I might have broken my neck!" Mr. Olsen declared angrily.

Stepping carefully past him down the stairs, I knelt down to examine the wire more closely.

"Look—it's been fastened to the side of the staircase with thumbtacks," I said. "A booby trap?" Mr. Olsen gasped.

"It looks like it," I told him, getting to my feet. I could feel my temper rising. Who would be so cruel?

"You probably saved my life, Nancy," Mr. Olsen said then. "I'm more grateful than you realize."

I blushed. As I said before, praise always makes me feel self-conscious. "Well, at least I prevented you from having a nasty fall, Mr. Olsen. I'm beginning to think that the vandal—or vandals—wants you and your wife to leave Cardinal Corners."

Mr. Olsen nodded. "Well, I've thought so all along but didn't want to contradict Mrs. Fayne and Mrs. Mahoney. Still," he added, tapping his chin pensively, "if there was a mishap like this on Saturday, it could mean a serious lawsuit. And besides that, I wouldn't like to see anyone get hurt."

By the time we returned to the kitchen, George had the electricity on again. "Someone tampered with the fuse box, Nancy," she told me. "It's an old-fashioned kind, and the round fuses had been unscrewed. I doubt that a ghost did it."

I agreed. "Does Juan Tabo have any reason to have a grudge against you?" I asked the Olsens. "What about other B and B owners in the vicinity?"

The Olsens shook their heads. When I showed Mrs.

Olsen what I'd found on the staircase, she frowned with concern and immediately suggested that the tea party be postponed. "I don't want anyone to get hurt on our opening day of business," she said. "We can reschedule the event after Nancy finds the culprit."

Glancing out the window, I could see the rain continue to pour. I sighed heavily. Postponing the event was the last thing I wanted to do. Mrs. Fayne and the other committee members had done a lot of preparation and spent a lot of money on advertising. Besides, everyone was looking forward to it.

"Nancy has already figured out that there's no ghost," Mr. Olsen remarked. "I think we should give her another day or two at least to get to the bottom of this. She hasn't even had time to search the basement or walk around the yard."

"I agree with your husband," George told Mrs. Olsen. "Give Nancy another day or two. She'll solve the case. Trust me. There's no mystery too perplexing for Nancy Drew."

Mrs. Olsen was convinced by George's praise and my promise to return the next day. George and I stayed another hour looking around the house. I recommended a security firm that could quickly put in burglar alarms, and Mr. Olsen called to ask about installation. By then it was almost dinnertime. Mrs. Olsen graciously invited George and me to stay for pot roast, but we politely declined and promised to return the next day.

"The wire over the staircase—that is far worse than shattering teapots," George said as I drove her home. "Are you going to tell the committee what happened?"

"I don't know," I said, chewing my bottom lip. "Ms. Waters is already convinced the tea party should be canceled. I think this would cinch it for her. Are you going to tell your mom?"

"I don't know," George said. "She's already so worried."

Merging onto the highway, I got a quick glance at a tow truck on the side of the road and wondered if it was the one that belonged to my friend Charlie Adams. He's the AAA guy and has come to my rescue more than once when I've locked my keys in the car or needed a jump. He liked this sort of weather, he'd once told me. People drove too fast, and as a result they often drove off the road, into the nearest ditch. Drivers' carelessness was good for business, Charlie had explained.

"Let me talk to my dad first," I said. "I'll tell him everything that's been going on and get his opinion about what we should do. And then I'll call you, okay?"

George nodded. Like me, she trusted my dad

to give valuable advice. He isn't the most successful attorney in River Heights for nothing. I dropped George off, and by the time I reached my own home, I was starving and ready for a hot shower. I decided on the shower first.

Afterward Hannah had homemade clam chowder and fresh cheese biscuits waiting in the kitchen. She fussed over me until I sat down at the kitchen table and began eating. She said that my dad had already eaten and was working in his study. As I buttered a biscuit, I briefly told her about the committee's concerns and my escapades at the Olsens'.

"And now I'm so hungry I think I could eat three bowls of chowder," I declared, digging in.

Hannah beamed at me. She loves to see me eat. "Of course you're hungry!" she insisted. "What with ghosts and thunderstorms and all sorts of shenanigans going on at the old Rappapport place, you must be famished."

"What's all this about ghosts?" my dad asked, strolling into the kitchen. He was wearing jeans and a sweater and had a law book in one hand and his reading glasses in the other.

I smiled at him and repeated everything that I'd just told Hannah. I also told him about the discussion at Mrs. Fayne's earlier that day. Dad listened carefully. Occasionally he frowned. When I showed him the two thumbtacks and length of thin wire I had in my purse, his frown deepened.

"I don't like it, Nancy," he said. "This sort of thing is more than just an adolescent prank. Someone intended to commit bodily harm."

"I know," I said. "Mrs. Fayne thinks someone is trying to sabotage Saturday's fund-raiser, but the Olsens are afraid someone is trying to keep their bed-and-breakfast from opening on time. After this incident on the staircase, I think they may be right."

I ate another spoonful of chowder and added, "Of course, their maid thinks the house is haunted. She insists that a ghost is responsible for all that's happened." I smiled and shrugged. "But I've never heard of a ghost tampering with a fuse box."

"The old Rappapport place was never haunted before," Hannah said dismissively. "Who is the maid?"

"A woman named Emily Spradling," I told her.

"Emily Spradling!" Hannah declared. "She's a silly creature—and she's got four silly sisters, too. They take after their mother—very superstitious and timid," she added knowingly. "If they'd lived in Jane Austen's day, they'd be the swooning type."

I chuckled. I could easily imagine Emily fainting and falling to the floor in a heap.

"Nancy, the ghost stories aside, this could be a

very dangerous case," my dad put in. "There might be a real criminal behind all this. I want you to be careful."

I nodded and helped myself to another warm biscuit. "This case is pretty perplexing," I said. "Why run the Olsens out of business—if that's the motive behind the pranks? And are Emily or Juan involved?"

"You've solved tougher mysteries than this one," my dad said with a smile.

I appreciated my dad's confidence in me, but something was worrying me, too. "So, Dad, do you think I should tell the planning committee about the staircase incident? I'm afraid if I do, they will cancel the event. On the other hand, if I don't and someone gets hurt on Saturday, I'd never forgive myself."

"I think you're obligated to tell both Mrs. Fayne and Mrs. Mahoney what happened this afternoon," my dad said. "I think Chief McGinnis should be informed as well. And I want you to promise that you won't go to Cardinal Corners alone," he added, placing his hand on my shoulder.

"George and I are going back there tomorrow afternoon," I told him. "I'll be careful. I promise."

"Do you think the committee will cancel the tea?" Hannah asked, wiping her hands on a dish towel.

"I don't really know," I confessed.

"I hope not," Hannah said. "I've been looking forward to it. And I volunteered to be in charge of door prizes, you know."

I nodded. If I didn't solve the mystery soon and the committee canceled the tea party, there'd be a lot of disappointed library patrons in River Heights. The pressure was on!

I discussed a few more things with Dad, and when he returned to his study, I enjoyed a slice of Hannah's homemade carrot cake with thick cream cheese frosting. Then I called George and told her to tell her mother everything that had happened. I could tell she was relieved.

"Let's have lunch tomorrow with Bess after our dress fitting. Then we can all go out to Cardinal Corners," I suggested.

George eagerly agreed to the plan, and after saying good night, I called Mrs. Mahoney. I told her everything that had happened. She was shocked.

"Nancy, thank heavens you're all right!" she declared. "And poor Karl Olsen—he could have broken his neck!"

Outraged, she rattled on a bit about how important it was for me to stay on task and bring the culprit to justice.

Finally I interrupted her. "Are you going to cancel Saturday's tea, Mrs. Mahoney?" I asked. "Mrs. Olsen thinks it would be a good idea to at least postpone it until we catch the vandal."

After a long silence, Mrs. Mahoney replied. "I want to give you two more days, Nancy. If anyone can get to the bottom of this, it's you. I'm counting on you, Nancy." I sensed the urgency in her voice.

"I'll do my best, Mrs. Mahoney," I said. "I'm going back out there tomorrow to have another look around."

Later, when I crawled into bed, I realized that I had mixed feelings about Mrs. Mahoney's decision not to cancel the tea. Part of me was relieved. I wanted to wrap things up before Saturday. Another part of me was really worried. What if I didn't catch the culprit and someone got hurt?

I lay there restless for a long time. It seemed like I had just slipped into a sound sleep when the jangling of the phone on the nightstand by my bed woke me up.

"Hello?" I mumbled, brushing the hair from my eyes.

"Nancy Drew?" The voice was muffled.

"Yes, this is Nancy Drew," I said, propping myself up on my elbow.

"Stay away from Cardinal Corners," the voice growled, "or you'll be sorry!"

5

Tea for Two

N ow I was definitely awake. "Who is this?" I demanded.

There was a click and a dial tone. The caller had hung up. The phone on my night table didn't have caller ID, so I quickly pressed *69 to find out the caller's number. Unfortunately I had no luck that way, either. The guy who'd given me the threatening wake-up call must have been using a pay phone or phone card.

I was wide awake and my blood was pumping fiercely through my veins. What a way to start the day, I thought as I tumbled out of bed. I smelled the delicious aroma of French toast, bacon, and coffee coming from downstairs, and dressed quickly—in my oldest jeans. I knew I'd be exploring the Olsens' cellar and I might have to do it on my hands and knees. Hurrying to the kitchen, I gave Hannah a quick hug as I took my place at the breakfast table.

"Hmm, smells wonderful. Where's Dad?" I asked, pouring myself some orange juice.

"He ate bright and early and went straight to the office. Working on a big case," Hannah said, bringing coffee to the table. "But he said if you needed him for anything, don't hesitate to call. He also said to remind you to be careful," Hannah added.

"I will be," I promised. "I've got a busy day ahead of me, and it started off with a bang, too," I added, helping myself to the bacon.

When Hannah asked me what I meant, I told her about the phone call.

"Oh, Nancy," Hannah said, horrified. "This is getting more dangerous all the time! I'm sorry I didn't hear the phone ring. I must have been outside bringing in the newspaper from the porch. What are you going to do?"

"Exactly what I planned for today," I told her. "I'm going to see Chief McGinnis at the police station. I also have a fitting at Julia Jute's for my tea party costume, and then I'm having lunch with George and Bess," I told her. "After that, I'm going back out to Cardinal Corners."

"But not by yourself, I hope," Hannah said.

I shook my head. I'd promised my dad I wouldn't go out there alone, and I always keep my promises. "Mrs. Mahoney is counting on me to solve this mystery by tomorrow so she won't have to cancel the tea," I said. "There's no time to lose."

"A cancellation would disappoint so many people," Hannah agreed. "But don't take any chances. The committee can always postpone the event for another time—after all this is cleared up."

As soon as I'd finished my breakfast, I left for the police station. Driving down the street, I was delighted to see how sunny it was. The sky was blue; the trees were in full bloom. Except for an occasional puddle, you'd never guess there'd been a total downpour the day before.

"Sure hope the sun keeps shining," I muttered to myself. I had lots to do today and wanted the weather to cooperate.

My first stop was the River Heights Police Department. Chief McGinnis was standing in the corridor talking to some patrolmen when I walked in. He saw me immediately, straightened up, and sauntered over.

"Nancy Drew!" he exclaimed. "I guessed you'd be paying me a visit. No doubt you're looking into the teapot scandal." He chuckled and folded his arms across his chest.

"Teapot scandal?" I said, raising my eyebrows. "You

mean the act of vandalism that took place at Cardinal Corners?" I wanted him to know I took my cases seriously, even if he didn't.

The smirk slipped from his face and he said, "I'm afraid I can't help you. We've got no leads, no eyewitnesses, and no signs of breaking and entering. Nothing."

I nodded and bit my bottom lip. I'd expected as much.

"It's really out of my hands until the Olsens file charges, and then they're going to have to file charges against someone in particular," the chief went on. "Do you have anything you want to tell me?" He looked at me rather suspiciously.

"Actually I do." I retrieved the wire and thumbtacks from my purse and told him what had happened yesterday afternoon at the B and B. When I told him that Mr. Olsen could have tripped down the stairs and been seriously hurt, he cleared his throat nervously.

"This looks like the work of a pro," he said. "Perhaps I should send a squad car out there."

"That's a good idea," I told him. "I'm expecting something else to happen . . . maybe even today."

"Why?" he asked, glaring at me.

I told him about my threatening phone call early that morning and that the fund-raising committee was counting on me to get to the bottom of the mystery before Saturday.

"I'm working under a bit of a time crunch," I said. "I also promised my father I'd take every precaution. It would be a relief to see a police car patrolling the area, Chief McGinnis. I think the Olsens would feel safer too. If I turn up any clues this afternoon, I'll definitely let you know," I promised.

Chief McGinnis only grunted, but he seemed to relax a little and promised to send out that police car to the Olsens' right away. Good thing I mentioned my dad, I thought. Everyone knew and respected him, including the police.

"It would be a shame if the committee decided to cancel the fund-raiser," I went on. "So many people in River Heights are looking forward to it. It's a benefit for the library, you know."

"Sure," he said. "I heard about it." He shifted from one foot to another. He seemed uncomfortable.

"I really appreciate your help," I told him as I got ready to leave.

I was nearly to the door when he called out, "Nancy, just so you know, we did do a background check on the Olsens and their two employees and came up with nothing. No criminal records. Not even a speeding ticket," he added with a shrug.

"Thanks again," I replied. "If I turn up anything, I'll let you know."

"You do that," the chief replied, but I had the feeling

he didn't expect me to turn up anything important.

I hurried back to my car, reflecting on what Chief McGinnis had just told me. Emily Spradling and Juan Tabo did not have criminal records, but that didn't mean they weren't capable of mean tricks. They could even be con artists who'd never been caught. And if someone was trying to run the Olsens out of business, they might have bribed Emily or Juan to help them. I'd even considered the possibility that the gardener and maid may have hatched a plot together—to get revenge on the Oslens, maybe? I decided to stop briefly at Ms. Waters's house to discuss these possibilities with her.

I found her in the garden. She wore gardening gloves, a smock, and a broad hat to protect her face from the sun. She was kneeling beside a flower bed filled with yellow and purple pansies.

"Good morning, Nancy," she called out. I raised my hand and smiled.

"When I see your garden, I know where the old saying 'April showers bring May flowers' comes from," I said, walking through the gate.

She chuckled and stood up slowly. "Last night was more of a downpour than a shower. I was afraid I'd lost most of my new blooms," Ms. Waters said.

"Everything looks beautiful," I declared.

She smiled.

"I'm in charge of bouquets for the tables," she said, "so I wouldn't want anything to happen to my flowers—if there's still going to be a tea party," she added hesitantly.

"Everything will go as planned if I have anything to say about it," I assured her.

"Agnes Mahoney called me last night," she said. "She told me what happened at the Olsens'. Thank goodness you were there, Nancy! Karl Olsen could have had a serious accident."

When I presented my various theories to her, including the one about Emily and Juan Tabo possibly getting revenge on the Olsens, Ms. Waters opened and shut her mouth a couple of times before saying, "Wait! I think I need a cup of tea. Come into the house."

Following her to the living room, I couldn't help noticing the book on a large, overstuffed chair near the window: *Lady Susan* by Jane Austen. Who else? Everyone in town was reading one of the author's novels, it seemed.

"You know, tea wasn't such a social ceremony in Jane Austen's day as it was years later when Victoria was queen of England," Ms. Waters told me. She poured a cup of steaming hot tea for each of us.

"Still, Agnes insisted we call the fund-raiser the Jane Austen Tea Party because Miss Austen is so popular," she added.

I only nodded. I didn't know much about the history of tea drinking. Frankly I didn't care. I had a mystery to solve and wanted to get it done quickly. I tried to steer my hostess back on track.

"What if someone is trying to get the Olsens to leave Cardinal Corners?" I suggested as I picked up my teacup and looked at her expectantly.

"Nancy, I would never have thought of anything like that. No wonder Mrs. Fayne wanted to call you in on the case. You're so clever!" She beamed at me approvingly.

"Well, it's only a theory," I admitted. "I'm going out there again this afternoon. But I'm trying to explore all the possibilities. Someone may want to scare the Olsens out of business. That's the likely truth behind Emily Spradling's ghost story."

Ms. Waters shook her head slowly and muttered something that sounded like "That silly woman."

"Could you do me a favor?" I asked. "It relates to the case, of course."

"Of course," Ms. Waters replied. "What can I do?"

"Would you contact Luther Eldridge and find out if there are any old ghost stories about the Rappapport place, or stories of hidden treasure or anything like that?" I asked.

Mr. Eldridge was a reclusive amateur historian. There's not an old story or anecdote about River

46

Heights that he doesn't know. Between his knowledge of local history and what Ms. Waters has learned from a lifetime of working with books in the local library, they were bound to uncover any little-known tale that might help me with the case.

"I have so much to do today," I explained to Ms. Waters. "I just won't have time to stop by to see him, and I need all the help I can get."

Ms. Waters agreed to talk with Luther. "I'll even invite him for lunch," she said. "But to be honest, Nancy, I have a hard time imagining Emily Spradling being a part of any dishonest scheme. She's too high-strung."

I laughed and said, "I know what you mean. But here's my dilemma." Holding up a finger, I continued. "One, she's faking the whole scaredy-cat bit and is part of a scheme against the Olsens, or two"—and I held up a second finger—"she really thinks she's heard a ghost, which means *someone* wants to scare her out of her wits and that someone is using Emily for his—or her—own purposes."

"That would be easy," Ms. Waters said with an emphatic nod. "Emily would make a very convenient pawn. Any little thing would frighten her. She's not a very sensible woman, I'm afraid."

I nodded. "That's just what Hannah told me. Do you know anything about her husband?" I asked. "She mentioned him last night."

"Doug? He works as an orderly at the nursing home, Fern Terrace, I believe," Ms. Waters said. "Big strapping fellow, but not the brightest crayon in the box," she added, with a smile tugging at the corners of her lips.

I grinned. "So, not a likely pair to attempt to run the Olsens out of business?"

Ms. Waters shrugged. "Why should they want to?" she asked, leaning slightly forward.

"It's only another idea that needs exploring," I replied. "And at this point, I'm open to all possibilities." Glancing at my watch, I realized I needed to get going. "I'm going to be late for my fitting with Julia Jute if I don't hurry," I said. I thanked Ms. Waters for the tea and for her help.

Ms. Waters smiled and said, "I'll call you later this evening about my conversation with Luther Eldridge."

It was a little after eleven when I parked my car near the curb and dashed up the sidewalk to ring Julia's doorbell. I found the front door standing open, however, and after tapping tentatively, I let myself in.

I could hear voices—all female—coming from a room down the hall, and I made my way toward them. Stopping on the threshold of the first bedroom on the right, I was amazed by something I'd never seen before: my friend George in a long, old-fashioned white dress with puffy sleeves. She was standing on a stool, looking annoyed.

"Nancy, you're late!" she snapped.

6

Pride and Prejudice

Late *again!*" **Bess Marvin** declared, emerging from the bathroom. She wore a blue dress similar to her cousin's white one. It made Bess's blue eyes seem even bluer and complemented her blond hair and rosy complexion to perfection.

"Nancy, come in," Julia said. She glanced up from George's hem to greet me with a warm smile. "We've been expecting you."

Julia Jute is about the same age as my father. Her short dark hair, streaked with gray, is always stylishly cut. She does tailoring for several department stores in town and a couple of the dry cleaners, too. When she heard about the Jane Austen Tea Party, she volunteered to alter the Regency-style dresses donated by the local theater group for those of us serving at the event.

"The gowns are beautiful!" I declared. "George, you look like a different person all dressed up like that." George, who towered over me on the stool, simply scowled.

Then, turning to Bess, I added, "And you're supermodel gorgeous, as always, Bess. That's such a lovely shade of blue." I started to say something about how authentic the costumes appeared to be when I heard someone stepping up behind me in the doorway. I turned and was slightly surprised to see Deirdre Shannon.

"Nancy, you're late," she mimicked.

George's scowl deepened, and she muttered something under her breath. She was in a sour mood because of Deirdre, I guessed. George doesn't like her one bit. None of us really like her. And to be honest, Deirdre doesn't like us, either. Come to think of it, she doesn't like very many people at all. Still, I try to be nice whenever we meet. We've known her since elementary school—back then everyone called her DeeDee.

Stepping aside so she could enter the room, I said, "That soft green color is a very becoming shade on you, DeeDee. It really brings out the color of your eyes."

Deirdre snorted at my compliment and shrugged past me. "It's Deirdre, not DeeDee," she corrected in a haughty tone. "And it's a frock, not a dress. Julia says that's what they were called in Jane Austen's time."

Deirdre immediately made her way to the long mirror on the far side of Julia's sewing room. She practically pushed Bess out of the way so she could admire her own reflection. Even though Deirdre isn't a very nice person, she *is* quite pretty with her long, curly dark hair, green eyes, and very fair skin.

"Dress, frock, whatever! This is so humiliating," George moaned. "I can't believe I let you talk me into this, Bess."

"Oh, stop whining," Bess ordered, inspecting the puffed sleeves of her own frock. "You look like you stepped right out of the pages of one of Jane Austen's novels."

"You'll like the jacket, Georgia," Julia said.

Deirdre snorted at the seamstress's use of George's full name, but I noticed that her green eyes widened with envy when Julia retrieved a smart red jacket from the back of a nearby chair.

"Step down and try this on," Julia said to George. "This is called a spencer. Your cousin said you preferred a more tailored style in clothes, so I thought I'd include this as part of your costume."

George stepped down from the stool and slipped on the jacket. It was ruby red and short waisted with long sleeves. "I *do* like this," George admitted.

"So do I," Deirdre spoke up. "I want one just like it."

"You can hardly wear a red spencer with your green frock," Bess said, rolling her eyes and emphasizing the word *frock*. "You'd look like a Christmas tree. Nancy, this one's yours." Bess held up a creamy apricot-colored frock. "Go slip it on so Julia can pin up the hem."

"You're next, Deirdre," the seamstress said. "Up on the stool, please."

While Julia turned her attention to Deirdre, I took my dress—I mean, *frock*—and slipped into the bedroom to try it on. After a minute or so, Bess poked her head around the door.

"Need someone to zip you up in the back?" she asked.

I nodded. "This is beautiful and surprisingly comfortable," I said, smoothing out the skirt of the gown with one hand.

"Nancy, stand up straight," Bess ordered, fussing with my zipper. "I knew this color would be perfect for you. It brings out the reddish gold highlights in your hair," she added.

When we stepped out of the bedroom and joined the others, Bess added, "This style was all the rage in Jane Austen's day. But of course, back in 1806, there would have been dozens of little buttons up the back instead of a zipper."

"Have you altered a gown for yourself?" I asked Julia.

"Yes," Julia replied after removing a pin from her mouth. "And one for Mrs. Mahoney, Ms. Waters, and even Mrs. Olsen. I took that one out to her on Sunday and made her try it on, just to be sure everything fit comfortably." Then, raising her eyebrows a bit, she added chattily, "There was quite an argument going on in the kitchen when I was there."

"Between Mr. and Mrs. Olsen?" I asked, intrigued.

"No, Karl was arguing with the gardener, who had insisted on a raise. Karl told him no. Apparently the gardener has quite a temper," she added with a knowing wink.

"Hmm, that's interesting," I said. I recalled the expensive watch Juan had been wearing the day before.

"Carol Olsen was embarrassed, of course," Julia chattered on as she returned attention to Deirdre's hem.

"Did you hear what they said exactly?" George asked.

"No, but Nancy could find out easily enough," the seamstress replied, looking over at me with a smile. "You're so clever."

Deirdre snorted then and rolled her eyes. With a touch of impatience, she said bluntly, "I want a jacket like the one you've picked out for George." She stood on the stool holding her arms out to the side and looking down at Julia Jute with something between a glare and a smirk.

Seeing the seamstress blush with discomfort, I hastened to change the subject. "I sure hope we don't have to wear high-heeled boots with lots of buttons on the side. We'll be on our feet most of the afternoon. I want to be comfortable."

"I don't want to twist an ankle or slosh cups of hot tea all over," George added.

I chuckled. I'd been worrying a little about the same thing. "I can be kind of a klutz too," I admitted.

"So we've noticed," Deirdre commented dryly.

Both Bess and George gave Deirdre a dirty look. I chose to ignore her.

"I suggest you wear ballerina flats, if you have them," Julia said, looking up from Deirdre's hem. "Or even a pretty pair of slippers."

"We can all be thankful none of us have to wear pattens," Bess put in.

"What are pattens?" I asked, studying my reflection in front of the long mirror.

"That's what they wore on rainy days in Jane Austen's time to keep their shoes dry and the hems of their long dresses from dragging in the mud," Bess said. "They were overshoes with thick wooden soles supported by large metal rings on the bottom. They raised you off the ground a few inches, out of the puddles. Just imagine all those women going *cling-clang* down the muddy streets of London and Bath," she added.

Leave it to Bess to know about fashion trends—even the ones that were in hundreds of years ago!

"You may step down now, Deirdre," Julia said. "Your frock fits perfectly."

"What about a jacket like the one George is wearing?" Deirdre asked again.

There was a brief, uncomfortable silence before Julia said, "There's only one like it in the collection the theater group gave me. But perhaps you'd like to wear this." She retrieved a garment from the closet. It was made from some gauzy white material and looked like a long sleeveless vest.

"Is that a pelisse?" Bess asked.

"It is," Julia admitted. "It was a very popular clothing accessory in Jane Austen's day."

"I don't like it," Deirdre said with a pout.

"But I do!" Bess exclaimed. She shot Deirdre a scathing scowl and then turned to admire the pelisse. Her cheeks were bright red. I could tell that Bess was angry. She's a very tenderhearted person, and I knew she was afraid that Deirdre had hurt Julia's feelings.

"May I try it on?" Bess asked politely.

"Certainly," Julia said. She helped Bess slip the

pelisse over her blue frock. She looked quite stunning. With her blond hair and sparkling blue eyes, Bess is a head turner, that's for sure—even in old-fashioned clothes.

While we *oohed* and *aahed* over the addition to Bess's costume, Deirdre flounced out of the room. She doesn't like anyone being the center of attention—unless, of course, it's her.

"Your turn, Nancy," Julia said, turning to me with a smile. Her face was slightly flushed. I felt embarrassed by Deirdre's rudeness, but I could tell that Julia was pleased that Bess liked the pelisse.

I was standing on the stool having my hem measured when Deirdre came back in wearing a pair of flared jeans and a pink and orange peasant blouse.

"When can I come back to pick up my frock?" she asked Julia.

"Any time Thursday afternoon or Friday," Julia replied. "I'll have your gown hemmed, washed, and pressed by then."

"Thanks," Deirdre said—rather curtly, I thought. She turned to go and then suddenly stopped.

Placing her hands on her hips, she said to no one in particular, "Is it true that women in Jane Austen's time used to wet down their dresses and the slips underneath so the fabric would be more clingy?"

I glanced down at Julia, who looked up at me with

wide, astonished eyes. I raised my eyebrows questioningly and she shrugged.

"Some women did that," Bess spoke up, stepping away from the mirror where she'd been admiring her pelisse. "But it was considered quite scandalous. I mean, look how thin this material is!" She indicated the length of blue material that draped in front of her. "If it gets wet, you can practically see thought it."

Deirdre laughed. "I might just have to try it. A damp, clingy frock would certainly show off my figure," she added with a giggle.

"You wouldn't dare!" George taunted.

"Of course I would," Deirdre said. "I want to look particularly alluring on Saturday. I have a date for the tea." She looked up at me and smiled in a smug sort of way.

"I thought you were serving, like the rest of us," Bess said.

"I am," Deirdre replied, her green eyes never leaving mine. "But that doesn't mean I can't have a date, too."

"So who's the lucky guy?" George asked, in a sarcastic tone.

Deirdre gave me a coy smile. Then, turning to the door, she said over her shoulder, "Ned Nickerson."

7

Bullet Pudding, Anyone?

We'd left Julia Jute's house and were munching chips and salsa at my favorite Mexican restaurant, waiting for our order of cheese enchiladas, before Bess and George said anything about Deirdre.

"Nancy, I hope you don't believe what Deirdre said about going to the tea with Ned," Bess said, shaking her head. "I sure don't." She stabbed a tortilla chip into the salsa bowl.

"Deidre is lying, plain and simple," George agreed emphatically.

I smiled as I took a sip of my soda. Ned is my boyfriend, and he has been since we were in junior high. He's tall and good-looking, so girls are always saying he's cute and trying to get his attention. I'm used to it, but Bess and George have always been annoyed by Deirdre's flirty behavior around Ned. Frankly it bothers them more than it bothers me. I trust Ned. Besides, he doesn't like Deirdre. He's told me so. He thinks she's spoiled and selfish. And she is. Ned, on the other hand, has the sweetest dimples when he grins, and he's so much fun to be with. He's considerate, too. I can almost forgive Deirdre for trying to get her claws into him. *Almost.*

"Has Ned mentioned anything about going on Saturday?" George asked. She leaned forward slightly.

"No, he hasn't said a word about it," I replied. "But you and Bess don't have to try to cheer me up or anything. I'm *not* worried."

The waitress appeared with our platters of steaming enchiladas. We began rearranging our glasses and the basket of chips to make more room on the table. Then my cell phone rang. It was Ned.

"Hey, we were just talking about you," I said lightly.

"I hope it was all good stuff," he answered.

I told him what Deirdre had said about going to the tea with him on Saturday. He sputtered angrily before explaining that he was simply giving Deirdre, Mrs. Shannon, and his mother a ride to the event.

"And I have a little surprise for you on Saturday too," Ned added on a lighter note. "My mom says you're going to love it."

"Give me a clue," I urged.

"No way!" he declared with a slight laugh. "You'll just have to wait and see." Then he said he had to go. He was on his way to his Russian literature class.

After telling Bess and George what Ned had told me, I smiled and said, "Can we please change the subject now?" Reaching for the hot sauce, I asked George if she'd told Bess everything that had happened yesterday at the Olsens'.

"Fill me in," Bess urged.

While George gave a rundown of yesterday's incident, I started to dig in to my lunch. I was wondering what sort of surprise Ned had for me on Saturday when I realized that George was once again complaining about having to wear the long dress on Saturday.

"People seemed so prim and proper in Jane Austen's day," she said. "It's hard to believe that some women back then would wet their gowns to show off their figures."

"Jane Austen thought it was vulgar," Bess told her. "But she really wasn't a stuffy person. She had a good sense of humor and enjoyed a little silliness now and then."

"Like what?" I asked.

Bess smiled mischievously, revealing her dimples. "Like bullet pudding," she said.

"Bullet pudding?" George and I exclaimed in unison. Then we laughed. Bess laughed too.

"What in the world is bullet pudding?" I wanted to know.

"Sounds criminal," George added, putting down her fork.

So Bess explained how the British filled a large dish with flour, mounding it into a heap. Then they placed a bullet on the top of the mound. Everyone got a chance to slice into the flour. The unfortunate person who cuts the "pudding" when the bullet falls was expected to retrieve it—with her teeth!

"Can't you just see Jane Austen poking around in that mess with her nose and chin?" Bess laughed.

George and I howled with laughter.

"What a hilarious party game!" I declared. Turning to George, I added, "I hope your mom is planning on serving it."

"Yeah, I'd love to see Deirdre with flour all over her face," George said with a grin, helping herself to a sopaipilla from the basket the waitress had brought to the table.

"And up her nose!" Bess added with a giggle.

We shared a few more laughs, and then George added, "Well, I doubt bullet pudding is on the menu, but my mom *is* making some weird things for Saturday's tea."

"What kind of things?" Bess asked, taking a sip of her soda.

"Well, she made lots of little pie crusts for something called *treacle tarts*," George replied, wrinkling her nose. "And she's making something called *syllabub* too."

"*Syllabub?*" I repeated. "Sounds like a word game to me. 'Treacle' sounds like leaking motor oil or something."

Bess gave a hard, choking laugh and nearly snorted soda through her nose. George thumped her on the back. When she finally caught her breath, Bess explained. "*Treacle* is just an old-fashioned word for 'molasses.'"

"And *syllabub?*" I asked.

"I know what that is, too," Bess said. "It's a drink made with frothy cream or milk and flavored with cider and nutmeg. Sort of like egg nog."

"But my mom is serving it like pudding in small custard dishes," George explained.

Bess nodded. "You'll like it. Wait and see."

"I thought we'd be having scones with jam and little cucumber sandwiches," I said. "You know, the usual tea party snacks."

"Mom's making those things, too," George said. "She's really going all out. That's one reason she's so concerned about what's been happening at Cardinal

Corners. She doesn't want anything else to happen that might cause the other committee members to cancel the fund-raiser. My mom's got a lot invested in this event. She's donating all the labor and food and writing it off as advertising for her catering business. Hopefully she'll attract lots of new clients after Saturday's tea."

"Nancy, what can we do to help?" Bess leaned forward eagerly.

"I'm glad you asked," I said, shoving my plate to the side. "I want you to use your fix-it skills to disable a dumbwaiter, for one thing." Then I told them about my brief visit with Chief McGinnis and, later, with Ms. Waters. I also mentioned my anonymous phone call that morning.

Bess shuddered. "That creeps me out!" she declared.

"You've got to be extra careful, Nancy," George said.

"I will," I promised. "But I'm more determined than ever to find out what's going on out there at the B and B. It's not fair that Mr. and Mrs. Olsen should have some jerk frighten them away from their business, not after they've worked so hard for so long to save up money to open the place."

"Maybe it's the gardener," George suggested. "He seems liked a pretty surly guy, and Julia Jute said he was angry that he didn't get a raise."

"Yes, but Mrs. Olsen said he was a hard worker," I reminded her. "It could be Emily Spradling. Maybe she's really not as harmless and spacey as she seems."

"You mean, you think Emily could be doing all these pranks herself?" George asked.

"No one has seen or heard the ghost except her. She's even got a key to the house. She can let herself in and out without breaking and entering. She could be the one responsible for everything," I mused aloud.

"But why would she want to cause troubles for the Olsens?" Bess asked. "They've given her a job, for Pete's sake."

"I don't know," I admitted.

"There isn't much time to find out," Bess reminded me. "Today is Wednesday. The tea party is supposed to take place on Saturday afternoon."

"If it takes place at all," George added gloomily.

"The show must go on," I said, waving one hand dramatically. With the other, I reached for our tab. "Let's go! We've got a lot to do and no time to lose."

In the restaurant parking lot, I saw Charlie Adams with his emergency truck. From the look of things, someone had a dead battery, and Charlie was jumping the car. When he saw me, he waved.

"He's got a crush on you, Nancy!" Bess giggled in my ear.

"We're outta here," George said, adding that she and Bess would meet me at the Olsens'.

I sighed and mustered up a smile as Charlie came striding eagerly toward me.

"Hey, Nancy, how are you?" he asked. "I saw you yesterday turning onto Highway Four. That was some storm, wasn't it? It rained hard. I mean, it rained *really* hard. It rained so hard it could have strangled frogs."

I laughed. "I saw you too, Charlie. Looked like you were giving someone a tow." It was best to keep him talking about cars and trucks. Otherwise the poor guy would blush and stammer and get all tongue-tied. It was embarrassing. But what could I do?

Charlie nodded eagerly. "Yeah, some weird guy skidded off the road. Bright yellow car—one of those little Japanese imports. He said he wasn't hurt, but I think he must have conked his head when he skidded into the ditch. He wouldn't answer his cell phone when it rang—and it rang twice. He had lots of junk piled on the front seat. A real oddball." Charlie shook his head wonderingly.

"Well, good to see you again," I said lamely. "Take care."

"Are you on another case, Nancy?" he asked in a breathless rush as I turned to go.

"Yes, I am," I admitted. Then I pointed over his

66

shoulder. "Looks like your customer wants to speak with you."

The mechanic turned and saw the impatient businessman motioning for him to return. Charlie sighed. "Okay, Nancy, see you around," he said. "Bring your little hybrid in sometime so I can check the belts. Can't be too careful with belts."

I smiled and promised I would. Then I hurried to my car and made my way to Cardinal Corners. I was beginning to feel the time crunch with this case. I thought of all the food Mrs. Fayne had already made for Saturday's tea, and Julia's altered frocks and Hannah's door prizes. Chewing my bottom lip, I made up my mind not to waste a single minute the rest of the day. I had to figure out what was going on—and fast.

I caught up with George's vehicle on the highway. As soon as we made the turn on the frontage road to Cardinal Corners, I kept my eyes open for the squad car Chief McGinnis had promised to send. I didn't see one. I wondered if he forgot or simply hadn't bothered.

After turning into the driveway and parking behind George's car, I stepped out and waved at Mrs. Olsen, who came hurrying down the steps, looking pale and frightened.

"Oh, Nancy!" she called out. "Thank goodness you're here!"

8

Conked Out!

What's the matter, Mrs. Olsen?" I asked after hastily introducing Bess.

"I don't think I can take the harassment!" Mrs. Olsen's voice cracked and her shoulders drooped. It looked like her short red hair hadn't been combed since I saw her yesterday.

"Tell us what happened," Bess urged. She placed a comforting hand on the woman's arm.

"Last night more teapots were broken, despite the new security alarm, and we had a threatening phone call early this morning," Mrs. Olsen said. "I don't know who it was. Then Emily called in sick. Said she'd come down with the flu or something and wouldn't be in the rest of the week."

"Emily is lying," Mr. Olsen spoke up as he joined us in the foyer. "She's no sicker than I am."

I introduced Bess to Mr. Olsen. They shook hands. "Emily is scared," he added with a wry smile.

"After this morning's phone call, I'm scared too," Mrs. Olsen said.

"I told you we could rule out ghosts." I tried to sound cheerful. "Generally ghosts don't tamper with fuse boxes or make threatening phone calls. I got one too, warning me to stay away from here."

"Oh, Nancy, we can't ask you to keep working on the case now. It's too dangerous," Mrs. Olsen said with a worried frown.

"If you think an anonymous phone call can scare Nancy Drew off a case, you don't know her very well," Bess declared with a flush of pride. I cast a grateful smile in her direction.

"What did the caller say exactly?" George asked Mrs. Olsen.

"Did you recognize the voice?" I added.

"No, but it was a man's voice—deep and gruff-sounding," Mrs. Olsen replied. "He told us to leave Cardinal Corners *or else*."

"Whoever it is knows that you've called Nancy in to help," Bess noted. "How many people know that?"

"Good question, Bess," I said. "We'll have to think about that later and make a list of possible suspects. Right now I want to look around outside. I'd like to talk with Juan Tabo, if he's here today," I added.

"I'll come with you and show you around," Mr. Olsen offered.

"But what am I going to do?" Mrs. Olsen asked helplessly. "I can't possibly take care of everything that's got to be done for Saturday's tea without Emily, and my computer hasn't been working since yesterday's storm. I need to check if any customers made online reservations for the B and B. I don't know what to do," she said, throwing up her hands.

"Mrs. Olsen, let me look at your computer," George offered. "I might be able to help."

That's an understatement, I thought. There's hardly anything George doesn't know about computers. She's a genius! I've seen her hack into programs that are supposedly triple protected.

"After I get your computer up and running again, I'll call my mom," George added. "She has a list of kitchen assistants, pastry chefs, and linen service workers that she uses when she's hired to cater an event. I'll have her call someone to fill in for Emily for a few days."

"Could you?" Mrs. Olsen asked. Her face lit up.

"Sure, no problem," George said, and gave me a

sidelong grin. "She can even round up some teapots to replace the broken ones."

"Are you sure it won't take up too much of your mother's time?" Mrs. Olsen added. "I know how busy she is right now."

"No trouble at all," George assured her. "She has all the information right on her computer."

"George created the bookkeeping and filing system for her mom's catering business," I explained. "She does all Mrs. Fayne's scheduling and billing and even orders the supplies."

"I'm impressed!" Mr. Olsen declared. "Carol and I should hire you to organize our computer files, too."

"Sure thing," George agreed. "But first let's get that computer working again."

As Mrs. Olsen showed George the computer, Mr. Olsen led Bess and me out the front door and down the steps into the yard.

There were two bright red cardinals drinking water from a nearby birdbath—the same bird that the Olsens had named Cardinal Corners for. We made a slow orbit around the house, taking the time to check the flower beds and windowsills, looking for footprints or smudges of any kind. But if the vandal had somehow made his way into the house through any of the first-story windows after disabling the alarms, then the rain had washed away any evidence.

"There sure are lots of trees over there," Bess remarked. She pointed to the wooded area some distance from the house. "That would be a good place to hide," she added, reading my mind.

"The trees *are* pretty thick in there," I said. "Is that your property, Mr. Olsen?"

"Some of it," the older man admitted. "There's a little path that goes through the woods and down to the river. Then you're on county land."

"Any buildings back in there, like a storage shed or barn or something?" I asked.

Mr. Olsen shook his head. "Nothing but an old storm cellar," he replied.

We'd been strolling purposefully around the property when we came to a small green garden shed with a slanted roof. Juan Tabo was coming out of the shed with a pair of hedge clippers in one hand.

"Hey, Juan!" Mr. Olsen called out. The gardener looked up and scowled when he saw us walking toward him.

"I understand he got pretty upset when you refused to give him a raise recently," I said quietly.

Mr. Olsen looked surprised that I knew about this. He replied frankly, "We can't afford to give him a raise until we're officially open for business . . . and then only if things go well. Juan, come here," he called out.

Juan propped the hedge cutters up against the open door of the shed and strode over—reluctantly, I thought. His dark eyes flickered briefly over me and then lingered on Bess's face. His eyes widened a bit, and his mouth practically dropped open. I wasn't a bit surprised. Bess is gorgeous, as I've said before. Most guys are dazzled when they meet her for the first time.

When Mr. Olsen told him I had a question or two, Juan pulled his gaze from Bess's face and narrowed his eyes at me. "What about?" he snapped.

"Someone's sneaking into the Olsens' house and destroying private property," I told him. "Mr. Olsen wants me to find out who it is." Again I noted Juan's watch and promised myself I'd find out how he could afford it.

"I don't know anything," Juan said irritably. He took a step backward and folded his arms across his chest. "You think I did this thing?"

"Not at all," Bess spoke up. She gave Juan a beaming smile. "But Nancy needs to question everybody who might have seen someone sneaking into the house. Perhaps you've seen someone lurking in the woods."

Disarmed by Bess's warm smile and soothing tone, Juan appeared to relax. I took full advantage of my friend's effect on him and jumped in with another round of questions.

"Have you seen anything suspicious? Perhaps someone snooping in the garden shed? Any trampled bushes or flowers near the windows? Strangers parked on the road watching the house?" I asked.

Juan shook his head. "Sorry, I've seen nothing like that."

Turning to Mr. Olsen, I said, "And you haven't seen any strangers, have you?"

Before Mr. Olsen could answer, Juan snapped his fingers and said, "Wait, I suddenly remember!" His dark face lit up. "A yellow car—a small one—parked in the woods. Back there," he said, pointing, "near the river."

"A small yellow car?" I asked. My pulse began to race with excitement as I remembered my earlier conversation with Charlie Adams.

"Yellow like a marigold," Juan said with a vigorous nod.

"When was this?" I asked eagerly.

"Monday, for sure," Juan said. "And another day last week. I don't remember which. Is it important?"

"Yes, I think so," I told him. "This could be our first real lead."

"What were you doing down there by the river, Juan?" Mr. Olsen asked.

"I go down that way with my lunch sometimes. It's quiet in the woods," Juan added almost apologetically. "That's when I saw the car."

"Did you see the owner of the vehicle too?" Bess asked.

Juan shook his head. "I saw nobody. Just the little car."

"Thanks, Juan," I said. "You've been a big help. If you see the yellow car again, will you tell me or Mr. Olsen?"

He nodded. Then, casting one more admiring glance at Bess, he returned to the garden shed to retrieve his hedge cutters and resume his work.

"Bess, when I was talking with Charlie Adams in the parking lot after lunch, he told me he'd towed a bright yellow car near here yesterday during the storm," I said.

"You sound pretty excited, Nancy," Bess teased.

"I am," I admitted.

"Do you think the car that was towed is the same one that Juan saw?" Mr. Olsen asked.

"Well, bright yellow cars aren't all that common," I pointed out.

"Of course it could be the same car and still not have anything to do with the break-ins," Bess said.

"That's true," I replied. "But I have a hunch the car—and its owner—have something to do with what's been going on here."

"I've learned never to doubt Nancy's hunches," Bess said, turning to Mr. Olsen.

"Will you show us the storm cellar in the woods?" I asked.

With a shrug, Mr. Olsen led the way, explaining that the old storm cellar hadn't been used in years. The grass was still wet from yesterday's rain, and I was glad I'd worn my hiking boots instead of my pink Converse. They would have been soaked by now.

"There it is," Mr. Olsen said. He indicated two large wooden doors with rusty handles that seemed to cover a wide hole in the ground. Reaching for one of the handles, I gave a hard tug. The door opened with a groan.

"Looks like it hasn't been used for quite a while," Bess said, peering down into the darkness.

"It hasn't," Mr. Olsen said. "It's supposed to have been used as a safe haven from tornados and thunderstorms, but it's too far from the house," he added. "And it couldn't have been very convenient for storing homemade canned goods or surplus vegetables and fruits in the old days. One would have too far to go to fetch them. I can't understand why they put it way out here in the first place."

"You can see the house well enough from here," I said, pointing. "But when we were in the yard talking to Juan, we couldn't see this cellar. That means anyone sitting or standing here, where we are now, could watch the house without being noticed."

"You think that's what the owner of the yellow car has been doing?" Mr. Olsen asked.

"It seems likely," I replied.

"But you don't know that for sure," he went on. "I mean, there's no evidence."

"Then let's look for some," Bess suggested.

"Just what I was about to say!" I exclaimed. "Bess, you go that way, and Mr. Olsen, you go to the left. I'll take the footpath toward the river."

"But what are we looking for?" Mr. Olsen asked.

"Anything that might indicate someone's been here recently—litter, cigarette butts, footprints in the mud . . . ," I told him.

As we began our search, I kept my attention fixed on the ground in front of me. I was already planning to call Charlie to get a more thorough description of the yellow car he'd towed back to his shop yesterday—the one with the oddball driver, as he'd put it. There was a connection—I could feel it in my bones. I sure hoped Charlie had written down the license plate number.

Just then I noticed a bit of paper and bent down to pick it up. "What do you know?" I muttered to myself. It was a bubble gum wrapper. It looked fairly new, aside from being damp and slightly smeared with mud.

Glancing around quickly, I found a second discarded

wrapper, just like the first. As I bent down to retrieve it, I heard a twig snap behind me and a footstep or two. Thinking it was Bess or Mr. Olsen, I said, "Hey, look what I've found!"

That's when something came down hard on the back of my head. My knees gave way, and I crumpled to the ground.

9

Important Clues

Nancy, are you all right? Can you hear me?"

At the sound of Bess's voice, I opened my eyes with a flutter and saw my friend's anxious face peering closely into my own. As I regained consciousness, I became aware of the painful lump on the back of my head and realized that I was lying on the ground.

"I'll call an ambulance!" Mr. Olsen declared, peering down at me.

"No, wait! Please don't," I said weakly. "I'm fine. Really." With Bess's help, I sat up slowly. My clothes were damp from lying in the wet grass.

"What happened, Nancy?" Bess asked. "Did you trip and fall?"

"No, someone conked me on the head," I told her. I explored the tender spot at the back of my scalp with trembling fingers. "Ouch!" I exclaimed, pressing too hard on the lump.

"Did you see who it was?" Mr. Olsen asked.

I shook my aching head slowly. "No, I thought it was Bess coming up behind me," I admitted. "Then—*whammo!*"

"I'll take a quick look around," Mr. Olsen declared. He hurried off deeper into the woods toward the river.

"Help me up, Bess," I said. As I rose slowly to my feet, supported by Bess, I suddenly realized that my hands were empty. I looked around on the ground at me feet.

"Hey, do you see any bubble gum wrappers?" I asked.

Bess shot me a skeptical glance. I could tell she was wondering just how hard I'd been hit on the head. "Bubble gum wrappers?" she asked hesitantly.

"I found two of them right here," I said. "I was bending over picking up the second one when I got clobbered."

"No, I don't see anything," Bess replied, glancing around.

"That's weird," I muttered. "Why take the wrappers?"

"Incriminating evidence?" Bess suggested. She arched her brows. "An important clue?"

"I think you're right," I agreed. "Someone has been trespassing on the Olsens' property, and whoever it is chews strawberry-flavored bubble gum."

Mr. Olsen returned then. He was panting heavily, and I knew he'd been running. "I didn't see anybody down that way, and no yellow car, either," he announced. Then, noting that I was on my feet again, he asked anxiously, "Nancy, are you sure you're all right? You might have a concussion. Or perhaps you need stitches," he insisted.

"I'll be fine," I replied. But to satisfy him, I bent my head down and let Bess examine the lump. When she declared that there was no gaping wound, Mr. Olsen reluctantly quit pressing me to see a doctor.

"At least come back to the house for an ice pack and a cold drink—or hot tea, if you prefer," he offered.

"That sounds good," I admitted, realizing suddenly how thirsty I was. "I need to make a phone call, too, and then I want to explore your basement."

Mr. Olsen shook his head admiringly. "You've got spunk, Nancy Drew! That much is certain."

Back at the house, we found George and Mrs. Olsen laughing together while they enjoyed a snack in the kitchen. George happily informed us that the computer was working again and domestic help was on the way. But when Mrs. Olsen heard about my misadventure, the smile slipped from her face. She hovered over me with concern.

"Perhaps we should take you to the emergency room," she suggested.

"Maybe I should drive you home," George said with a worried frown.

"No, really, I'm fine," I said, accepting a glass of raspberry lemonade from Mrs. Olsen. I knew they meant well, but I was beginning to get a little annoyed by everyone's concern.

"Who would do such a thing?" Mrs. Olsen asked fretfully.

"Could it have been Juan?" Bess asked. I shrugged and Mrs. Olsen gave a horrified gasp.

"Oh, I hope not!" she declared, looking even more concerned.

"Couldn't have been the gardener," George spoke up. "He's been trimming the bushes. I could see him from the window while I was working on the computer."

When Mr. Olsen told his wife about Juan spotting a yellow car in the woods, she gave another little gasp. "I don't like the idea of being spied on by someone hiding in the woods," she said nervously.

"Now, Carol," he said soothingly. "We don't know for sure that anyone is spying on us."

Bess and I exchanged glances. I gave her a warning

look. I didn't want her to mention the bubble gum wrappers—at least, not yet. Mr. Olsen may have had doubts about someone watching the house, but I didn't. I asked Mrs. Olsen if I could use the phone.

"Certainly," she said, and indicated the wall phone. This time I got a dial tone and called Charlie Adams at the mechanic's garage. He seemed delighted to hear from me again so soon and was more than willing to give me the name and address of the customer with the bright yellow car—as long as I promised not to tell where I'd gotten my information. He'd even written down the license plate number on the invoice.

"Is all this important, Nancy?" he asked. I could hear the hopefulness in his voice.

"Yes, very important," I assured him.

"Glad to help," he said with a happy sigh. "The guy sure was an oddball."

When he said "oddball," that reminded me of the other thing I wanted to ask him. "Hey, Charlie, you said something earlier about the weird things this guy had on the front seat of his car. What sort of things?"

Charlie rattled off a list: a golf club, pantyhose, several different-size flashlights, a small pair of binoculars.

"This may sound random, but any chance the guy was chewing gum?" I asked.

"Yeah, as a matter of fact he was, and he had a couple of packs on the dashboard and by the cup holder, too."

"Did you notice if it was strawberry flavored?" I ventured.

"It might have been," Charlie replied. "The packs had pink wrapping."

I then asked the mechanic for a brief description of the "oddball" and hung up the phone after expressing my heartfelt thanks for the helpful information. Turning, I found the Olsens and Bess and George staring at me inquiringly. They all seemed to be holding their breath.

"It must be good news," Bess declared with a smile. "Your eyes have that special gleam they get when you know you're on the right track."

"So what's up with the bubble gum?" George asked.

"It *is* good news," I said with a slight laugh. I explained the bit about the bubble gum wrappers and told them about Charlie's oddball customer.

"His name is Davy Reeve and he lives in River Heights." Turning to the Olsens, I asked, "Do you recognize that name?"

The couple shook their heads. "Like we told you before," Mr. Olsen said, "we're new here and really don't know many people."

"According to Charlie, he's short and has a red beard," I added.

Again Mr. and Mrs. Olsen just shook their heads.

"So, you think this Davy Reeve is the one who bopped you on the back of the head and swiped the bubble gum wrappers from your hand?" Bess asked.

I shrugged. "I'm not sure about that," I admitted. "Neither Mr. Olsen nor his gardener saw a yellow car down by the river today."

"But Reeve could have an accomplice," George suggested. I nodded. "And maybe one or both of them are small enough to get into the dumbwaiter," she ventured.

"Where is the dumbwaiter?" Bess asked.

"Over here," George said, indicating the small contraption. "This is where Emily says she heard the ghost yesterday afternoon—in here." George opened the door.

"A small person could get in there, I suppose," Bess said, examining the dumbwaiter. "And it looks easy enough to operate. There's even a manual pulley system so it can work without electricity."

"Really?" I asked, joining Bess and George to peer into the dumbwaiter. Bess showed me how it worked. Did I mention that Bess knows all there is to know about fixing things?

"Give me a screwdriver and I'll make sure the trespasser can't use this anymore," Bess assured the Olsens.

"So, the intruder could have tampered with the fuse box and slipped into the dumbwaiter without Emily noticing until it moved," Mr. Olsen said, retrieving a screwdriver from one of the kitchen drawers and handing it to Bess.

"But how did he break in to the house in the first place?" George asked.

"I still haven't figured that part out yet," I admitted. "We didn't find any trampled shrubbery around the house, and the windows haven't been tampered with either. And—"

I stopped short, interrupted by Bess's placing a finger to her lips and whispering, "Shush." She then pointed to the back door.

We all turned toward the door. Mrs. Olsen clutched her husband's arm. I made a motion for Bess and George to resume talking about the dumbwaiter while I tiptoed to the door. Grasping the knob, I turned it and pulled it open as hard and as fast as I could.

"Oh! Sorry. Ah, I—came to see Mr. Olsen. I—I—I . . ." Juan Tabo had been leaning so hard against the back door that he nearly fell over.

It was quite obvious to us all that he'd been eavesdropping.

10

Deep, Dark Secrets

What **do you think** you're doing?" I asked icily. I glared down at Juan, who stumbled to his feet and stood up as tall as he could, trying to regain his dignity.

"I came to speak with Mr. Olsen," he repeated, looking away in embarrassment.

"He was listening in!" George declared.

"I thought that sort of thing only happened in the movies," Bess said with a giggle.

"What do you want, Juan?" Mr. Olsen asked gruffly.

"I came to tell you that ... that ... I ..."

Juan gulped as I stared him down. He seemed to forget what he was going to say.

"Well?" I prompted him with a glare.

"I came to tell you that I'm done for the day,"

he finally managed to say. "I'll be back on Friday. I want to show you what I did with the debris from yesterday's storm."

"All right, I'll come with you," Mr. Olsen said, turning to go.

"Wait a minute," I said. "Not so fast, Juan. You were eavesdropping. Why?"

Juan flushed and looked down at the kitchen floor.

"Well?" I said sternly. I wasn't going to let him off the hook until I got an answer.

"I wanted to hear if you were talking about me," he finally admitted.

"And what if we were?" I challenged.

"Whatever that Spradling woman has told you about me, it isn't true!" Juan said defiantly.

Bess, George, and I exchanged glances. Talk about touchy! I thought. "What makes you think Emily Spradling has said anything about you to us?" I asked.

Juan hesitated. He looked from Mr. Olsen to Mrs. Olsen and then back at me.

"As far as I know, Emily has never spoken about you at all," Mrs. Olsen said. She sounded a little surprised.

"Why should she?" her husband asked, addressing his question to Juan.

"The woman doesn't like me," Juan said. "Her husband doesn't like me either."

"You've met Mr. Spradling?" I asked.

Juan nodded. "They came into my grandmother's restaurant once. I work there on weekends sometime."

"What makes you think the Spradlings don't like you?" Bess wanted to know.

Juan gave a shrug. "I can tell by the way she looks at me when I come into the kitchen," he said, frowning. "And her husband said that if I quit my job here at Cardinal Corners, he has a friend who wants to take my place." Then, looking at Mr. Olsen, he added, "But I don't want to lose my job here."

Mr. Olsen patted him on the back reassuringly. "You're not going to lose your job, Juan. Don't worry." Then, looking at me, he added, "I'll be back soon."

I nodded and watched the two men make their way out of the kitchen and down the back porch into the yard.

"Hmmm, I wonder if Juan's telling the truth," I murmured, thinking aloud.

"The fact that he was spying was definitely weird," George said.

"Makes me wonder if we can trust anything he told us earlier," Bess said pensively.

"Well, we know for sure that Charlie Adams

towed a yellow car, and the owner of that car chews bubble gum. That's a lead I intend to follow," I said. "But right now I want to get down into the basement and look around. Mrs. Olsen, will you show me the way?"

"Certainly," she said, and led us out of the kitchen to a door down the hall. At the top of the stairs, she flicked on the light and started down the steps. I thought it was pretty dim, so I pulled my trusty miniflashlight out of my pocket before descending the steps into the gloom.

"I'd feel better if you had a brighter bulb down here," I told her.

"If you've got one, I'll change it for you," Bess offered, coming down behind me on the stairs. George followed behind her. When we reached the bottom, I shook my head. The single lightbulb dangling overhead wasn't enough for us to thoroughly explore the basement.

"I think I have a one-hundred-watt bulb in a kitchen drawer," Mrs. Olsen said. "I'll go back and get it."

While she went back upstairs to the kitchen, I snooped around the basement a bit. So did Bess and George. We poked around in the corners and peered into boxes, old suitcases, and storage trunks.

"Here's the dumbwaiter closet," George said. She

touched a button and opened the small door. I peered inside with my small flashlight.

"Look!" I declared, aiming the beam on the inside wall. "There are muddy smudges in here."

"Must have been left by the intruder yesterday," George said. I nodded. Now I knew for sure that someone had been using the dumbwaiter to get from floor to floor of the old mansion. But how did the intruder get into the dumbwaiter in the first place?

We continued our search of the basement, but there wasn't much else to see except several shelves well stocked with canned goods, jams, and jellies and boxes of supplies like toilet paper and paper towels. All in all, it was neat and well organized.

"Hey, Nancy, look at this," Bess declared. I turned my flashlight beam in the direction she was pointing. Several jelly jars and some cans had fallen to the concrete floor. A few of the glass jars had shattered, leaving a sticky mess.

"Someone had an accident," Bess said. Efficient as ever, she quickly located an open roll of paper towels and began wiping up peach preserves from the floor.

"Do you think that Emily came down here, saw the so-called ghost, and dropped the jars?" George asked.

"I doubt it," I said, watching Bess clean up. "Emily couldn't have been carrying that many jars and cans all at one time."

"These metal shelves look pretty sturdy to me," Bess observed. "The jars couldn't have fallen off by themselves."

"Maybe someone bumped the shelves or tried moving them," George suggested.

"I'll bet you're right," I said, gripping one of the metal shelves. I tried to shake it but it didn't even wobble. The only way so many cans and jars could have fallen was if someone had pushed them over, as George suggested, or tried to move the shelves. "Seems like someone went to a lot of trouble to look behind here. I wonder why."

Mrs. Olsen came down the stairs, holding a new lightbulb. Mr. Olsen was with her. Bess handed the sticky paper towels to George and quickly retrieved a stepladder from the corner. Ms. Fix-it scrambled up nimbly and replaced the dim lightbulb with the brighter one. "Now, isn't that better?" Bess asked.

It was.

"Look at this mess!" Mrs. Olsen declared, seeing the broken jars on the floor for the first time. "What happened?"

"We think someone tried moving these shelves away from the wall," I told her.

"How odd!" Mr. Olsen said, bending over to pick up a small can of tomato paste. "Why would anyone do that? There's no wall safe or anything back there."

"What's in there?" I asked. I pointed to a small door on the far side of the basement. It was short and very wide and looked like the sort one might use for a kid's playhouse.

"Only a crawl space," Mr. Olsen explained. "We don't use it. Carol and I are too old to go crawling on our hands and knees," he added with a crooked smile. "But we do keep boxes of Christmas decorations stored just inside the door."

I gripped the old-fashioned doorknob and opened the door with a yank. "It's not locked," I said.

"Of course not," Mrs. Olsen said, mildly surprised. "We don't keep anything valuable in there. Why lock it?"

"Have you been rummaging around in these boxes lately?" I asked.

"No, why?" her husband replied.

"Have a look," I said. I stepped away from the short door so the Olsens could see.

"Oh my goodness!" Mrs. Olsen declared.

"Someone's been in here!" Her husband's tone was more than a little annoyed. The boxes of Christmas decorations had been rummaged through and strings of tree lights, extension cords, and wreaths were strewn around inside.

"How far back does the crawl space go?" George asked, kneeling down and peering in. I squatted down next to her and focused the beam of my little flashlight down the long narrow tunnel. It appeared to go on forever.

"I don't know, really. I've never explored it before," Mr. Olsen confessed.

"For all I know, it goes under the whole length of the house."

The hair on my arms was beginning to tickle. I had a hunch. Bess stepped up behind me and placed a hand lightly on my shoulder.

"Are you thinking what I'm thinking?" she whispered breathlessly.

I nodded as I examined the knob on the back side of the little door. There was a lock on the inside. Why have a doorknob with a lock on the *inside* of an empty crawl space?

"Don't even think about crawling in there, Nancy Drew!" George said looming over me with a frown. "You've already been conked on the head once today, and you promised your dad and Hannah that you would be careful."

"I need to find out just how far back this goes," I said, rising.

"Then I'll go," George offered. "Mr. Olsen, can I borrow your flashlight?"

While Mr. Olsen went upstairs to retrieve the flashlight, George and I worked out a plan. We sent

94

Bess upstairs too to get George's cell phone and mine from our cars.

"I want to stay in constant contact with you the entire time," I said. "And I want you to tell me if you see anything that looks suspicious."

"Girls, I'm not sure I approve of this," Mrs. Olsen said nervously. "We don't know what or who might be in there. What if something happens to you?" she said, addressing George. "I'd feel terrible. What would I tell your mother?"

"I'll be fine, Mrs. Olsen," George assured her. "This will be a piece of cake compared with some of the things I've done for Nancy before." George grinned at me.

I grinned back and repeated my orders: "Constant voice contact."

Once Mr. Olsen returned with the flashlight, and Bess with the cell phones, I checked the battery charge and made sure there was a signal on each phone. Then I dialed George's number. The ring sounded like someone sneezing violently. I grinned. "Are you ready?" I asked, speaking into the phone and looking at George.

"Ready as I'll ever be," George said into her phone.

"Be careful," Bess admonished her cousin. George nodded. Clutching her cell phone in one hand and the flashlight in the other, she got down on her hands

95

and knees and began crawling into the dark storage space. Bess and I knelt down in front of the open door while the Olsens peered over our shoulders. Mrs. Olsen clutched her husband's arm nervously.

"I have a feeling this is how the prowler is getting into the house," I told them, hoping that bit of information might cheer them up.

"But how? Where from?" Mr. Olsen asked.

"We'll soon find out," I replied. I knelt peering into the dark tunnel until I could no longer see George's feet.

"That's one deep crawl space," Bess declared.

"We had no idea it went back under the house so far," Mr. Olsen told us.

Although I could no longer see her, I could hear George's breathing and an occasional grunt over the cell phone. Sometimes she'd say "Ouch!" or "Whoops!"

She seemed to be crawling in the tunnel forever, although it had really been only a few minutes.

"Tell me, what do you see?" I asked, pressing the cell phone next to my ear as I sat down on the cold cement next to the little door. Bess quickly plopped down next to me.

"Nothing," came George's voice over the phone. Then I heard a slight gasp and George declared, "Nancy, you're never going to believe this!"

"What is it?" I asked, hearing the amazement in her voice. My heart skipped a beat. "What do you see, George?" I glanced up at the Olsens. They stared at me expectantly.

"I'm standing up!" George said.

"What?" I exclaimed. "You're standing up? In the crawl space?" I heard Mrs. Olsen gasp slightly. Bess murmured an amazed "Wow!"

"Yes, but it's not like a crawl space any longer," George went on. "It's an underground tunnel. Frankly, it's pretty darn big in here. I mean, you could move boxes and stuff, even small furniture," she added. "There are even a couple of places along the walls that have old electric light fixtures, but there aren't any lightbulbs now."

I repeated what George had said for the Olsens' benefit. Mrs. Olsen shook her head with amazement while her husband declared softly, "Oh my!"

"What else do you see?" Bess asked, talking into my phone.

"Cobwebs," came George's terse reply, "and a dead rat."

Bess shuddered. I wrinkled my nose. "Any sign that someone's used the tunnel recently?" I asked.

At first there was no response. The only thing I heard was crackling static. "George?" I said. "George, can you still hear me?"

97

"Oh no!" Mrs. Olsen said. She leaned toward me with an anxious look.

"Don't worry, Mrs. Olsen," Bess tried to reassure her. "Something is probably interfering with the phone signal. I'm sure my cousin is all right." Then Bess looked at me and raised her eyebrows inquiringly. I smiled and nodded. I wasn't worried. Not yet, anyway.

"George, can you hear me?" I repeated. "Say something, George." I hoped I didn't sound too anxious.

The static crackled and, finally, I heard George's voice cutting in and out. "All right . . . bricks . . ." Then there was nothing but silence. I repeated what she'd said to the others.

"What did she mean by 'bricks,' I wonder," Mr. Olsen said.

"I'm just glad she's okay," his wife put in. "She's been gone a long time."

"That may be what's causing the problem with the phone reception," Bess said. "It's hard to get reception inside brick buildings."

Mr. and Mrs. Olsen exchanged slight frowns. "Karl, do you think the tunnel is made of brick?" Mrs. Olsen asked. Her husband shrugged.

"I want to know where that tunnel goes," I said.

"She's been gone more than twenty minutes," Mr. Olsen announced after glancing at his watch. "Maybe you should tell her to turn around and come back."

"Let's give her another couple of minutes," I replied. "I'm sure she's all right and maybe—"

I didn't get to finish what I was going to say. George's voice came in loud and clear.

"Nancy!"

"George," I replied, sighing heavily. I was more relieved than I wanted to admit.

"Are you all right?"

"I'm fine," George said. "Can you hear me clearly now? I've reached the end of the tunnel."

"And where is the end of the tunnel?" I asked, glancing at Bess with an excited grin.

"Well, I can't say for sure," came George's reply, "but I think I may be in the storm cellar."

11

Smuggler's Hideaway

Still clutching my cell phone in one hand, I darted up the basement steps. Bess was right behind me. Together we dashed through the house, ran out into the yard, and sprinted across the sprawling lawns into the woods to the storm cellar Mr. Olsen had shown us earlier that afternoon. By the time the Olsens caught up with us, we'd already flung open the cellar doors and were peering down at George.

"See? I was right!" she declared, grinning up at us and waving her flashlight around wildly.

"Who would have guessed?" I said, grinning back at her.

"Tell George to be careful," Mr. Olsen warned. "Those old steps are pretty rickety. I don't even know if they'll hold up under her weight."

When Bess relayed this information, George said, "There's no need to use the steps. Someone thoughtfully supplied a brand-new rope ladder."

George nimbly climbed up and out. "I must admit, it's good to see daylight again," she said lightly. As she brushed the dirt off her jeans, the Olsens peered down into the cellar.

Shaking his head in amazement, Mr. Olsen said, "Well, now there's no doubt about how that sneak is getting into our house."

Bess removed a cobweb from the back of George's head while I briefly summarized. "Using this storm cellar as an entrance, he goes through the tunnel to your basement, hops into the dumbwaiter, and makes his way unseen from floor to floor of the house."

"But why, Nancy?" Mrs. Olsen asked, wringing her hands. "What is he looking for? If he wanted to rob us, he could have easily taken my computer, our camera, even my mother's silverware by now."

"I'm still working on that part of the puzzle, Mrs. Olsen," I replied.

"Oh, Nancy, I've got a present for you," George said, passing her flashlight to Mr. Olsen. "Hold out your hand."

When I did, she dropped a bubble gum wrapper into my palm. "Is it the same kind you found out here in the woods?" George asked hopefully.

I grinned. "It is! This proves that the person who has been watching the house from out here is the same one using the tunnel."

"Mr. Olsen, if you've got a basic padlock, we can make sure no one will ever use the storm cellar to sneak into your house again," Bess said.

"Unless he breaks the lock," I pointed out. When Bess only shrugged, I added, "But when he sees the lock, he'll know we're onto him."

We were making our way out of the woods back toward the house when Mr. Olsen said, "I wonder why the tunnel was built in the first place."

I was about to venture a guess when George pointed to the house and declared, "We've got company."

We all stopped and looked where she was pointing. A uniformed police officer was walking cautiously across the sprawling lawn toward us. From time to time, he looked to his left and then to his right. "Is everything all right, Mr. Olsen?" he called out.

Mr. Olsen waved and walked forward to meet him. "Yes, officer, everything is fine," he replied. "Nancy Drew and her young friends have just discovered how the intruder has been breaking in to our home."

The policeman's eyebrows shot up.

"I'm Nancy Drew," I said, stepping forward to introduce myself. "This is Bess Marvin and George Fayne. Did Chief McGinnis send you?"

"He did," the officer admitted. "We know about the break-ins and recent vandalism. The chief suggested I stop in and make a courtesy call."

"And check up on that nosy Nancy Drew," Bess whispered in my ear so the policeman couldn't hear. I tried not to smile but focused my attention instead on what the policeman was saying to the Olsens.

"My name's Madison. I was a bit worried when I knocked and no one came to the door," he told them. "Your cars are all parked out front, so I decided to look around inside. Even went upstairs. When I didn't find anybody, I thought I'd better come out here and have a look around. I'm glad everything is all right."

"It's more than all right," Mrs. Olsen said, smiling.

"The girls discovered a tunnel!" Mr. Olsen added. "Once we get a padlock on the doors of the storm cellar, the intruder won't be sneaking into our house anymore."

"No more broken teapots," Mrs. Olsen put in.

"A tunnel?" Madison asked with a confused look.

"George, will you show Officer Madison the secret tunnel?" Mr. Olsen asked. "I want to look for that padlock."

While George accompanied the policeman back to the storm cellar, Bess and I followed the Olsens into the house.

"I'm not waiting for Ms. Waters to call me about her conversation with Luther Eldridge," I said, briefly explaining to the Olsens what I'd asked the librarian to do for me. "I'm going to call him right now and find out what he knows about this old house and that secret tunnel."

At that very moment, the doorbell rang. "I'll get it," Mrs. Olsen said. When she returned to the kitchen, Luther Eldridge was with her.

"I was just trying to call you," I said, hanging up the phone.

"I'm not at home," Luther said with a shy grin. I laughed and formally introduced him to the Olsens. "As soon as Evaline Waters called and asked me a couple dozen questions about the old Rappapport property, I decided to drive out here," he added.

"Do you know anything about our place?" Mr. Olsen asked.

Actually, Luther knew quite a bit. He told us that at the turn of the century, the house belonged to a farmer named Leon Rappapport. Rappapport wasn't much of a farmer, and during the Prohibition years, he gave it up and became a bootlegger.

"He made and sold illegal booze," Luther explained.

"That was back in the twenties, right?" I asked.

Luther nodded. "Congress passed the Eighteenth

Amendment back in 1919. After that, it was against the law to make, sell, or transport intoxicating liquor in the United States. Leon Rappapport did all three," he said.

He then told us that when the Feds starting watching the house, Rappapport dug a tunnel underneath his property so he could transport the illegal whiskey down to the river's edge, where a waiting motorboat picked it up for distribution to his customers.

"What happened to Mr. Rappapport?" I asked. "The Olsens said this house was empty for years before they bought it."

"Rappapport went to prison for manslaughter," Luther told us.

"Manslaughter?" Bess declared.

"Yeah, that hooch he made was pretty awful. Apparently some of his bathtub gin was poisonous. People died," Luther said. "Anyway, Rappapport was still in prison when Prohibition was repealed in 1933. He died there—from liver trouble. Must have drunk too much of his own bad booze."

"They didn't call it 'rot gut' for nothing," Mr. Olsen put in.

I shuddered. The very words "bathtub gin" made my stomach lurch.

"So, did you find the tunnel?" Luther asked eagerly. "Evaline told me what's been going on out here."

Mr. Olsen filled him in on the details of the tunnel's discovery. When he was done, Mrs. Olsen said, "I wonder how the intruder knew about it. Prohibition was ages ago, and Mr. Rappapport's been dead a long time too."

"There are still a lot of old-timers in River Heights who might remember the tunnel. It was mentioned in the news stories about Rappapport's arrest," Luther replied. "Anyone who digs into the local history archives or old newspaper files would know too."

"So, what you're telling me is that there could be plenty of suspects out there," I said with a sigh.

Luther cleared his throat and said, "I'm afraid so, Nancy."

"Any idea why anyone would want to break in to this old place after all this time?" I asked him, taking a different approach. "Did the bootlegger keep all his money hidden in the tunnel or the basement somewhere?"

"They confiscated several thousand dollars when they made the arrest," Luther explained. "That was quite a stash in those days. The police found the money in old canning jars down in the basement."

"That explains why the intruder has been moving the shelves with the canned goods all around," Bess declared.

"And when he didn't find anything down in the

basement, he started exploring the rest of the house using the dumbwaiter," I added.

Luther's eyes lit up. "You have a dumbwaiter?" he asked, turning to the Olsens.

Mrs. Olsen smiled. "Indeed we do. Karl, show Mr. Eldridge the dumbwaiter while I put on some coffee."

Knowing that the Olsens would be busy satisfying Luther's curiosity for quite some time, I turned to Bess and said, "I feel a sudden urge to meet Charlie's oddball customer, Davy Reeve."

"Not without me," Bess insisted. "Your dad wouldn't want you going there alone."

I nodded, then scribbled a brief note for Officer Madison, telling him where we were going and asking him to relay the news about the tunnel's discovery to the chief. Mrs. Olsen promised to give the note to the police officer as soon as he and George returned to the house.

Bess and I made our way to Davy Reeve's apartment building. We took the elevator to the third floor and knocked, but no one was home. I wasn't really surprised. There was no bright yellow car in the parking lot.

"Try one more time," I said to Bess. She knocked harder. This time a door across the hall opened and a white-haired old woman peered at us from around the door.

"Mr. Reeve's not home," she said. "Don't usually get in before eight at night."

Bess and I exchanged quick glances. We both knew that a nosy neighbor could often be a great source of information.

"I was afraid of that when I didn't see his cute little yellow car in the parking lot," I said, smiling in a friendly way. She merely gave me a shrug and started to close her door.

"Has Davy shaved off his beard yet?" Bess asked cheerily. "I told him he should."

This time the woman opened her door wider and exclaimed, "I've told him he needs to shave that thing off too! A decent, respectable man should be clean shaven, and so I told him—more than once."

"We couldn't agree with you more," I said with a firm nod. Bess had luckily hit upon one of the woman's pet peeves, and I needed to take advantage of it. "Where's Davy working now? Do you know? Don't know who'd hire a man with a beard like that."

"He works at the old folks home," the woman said.

I stiffened. Quickly recalling the name of the home where Emily Spradling's husband was employed, I asked, "You mean Fern Terrace?"

"That's the one," she said with a brisk nod. When the woman started to launch into another tirade about bearded men, I interrupted her with a hasty thank-you and pulled Bess down the corridor to the elevator.

"Is that important—the nursing home?" Bess asked. "And how'd you know about it?"

"Ms. Waters told me that Emily's husband, Doug Spradling, works there," I replied.

"Hmmm, the plot thickens," Bess muttered. "Too bad Davy Reeve wasn't home. I know you have a long list of questions for him."

"Maybe Emily can answer one or two of them for me," I said. "Mrs. Olsen gave me her address earlier. Let's just stop by and see how she's doing. She did call in sick, remember?"

"She should be at home, then," Bess replied.

The street address Mrs. Olsen provided was not all that far from Davy Reeve's apartment. As we rounded the second corner, Bess gasped and cried, "Nancy, look!"

I slowed down and looked at where she was pointing. There, parked along the curb in front of Emily's house, was a little yellow car.

12

Nonsense and Sensibility

Just then my cell phone rang. It was Chief McGinnis. "Nancy, Officer Madison gave me your message, and I wanted you to know that we did that background check on Davy Reeve. The man's got a minor criminal record. I don't want you anywhere near the guy. Do you hear me?"

Ignoring his question, I asked one of my own. "Do you know that Mr. Reeve works at Fern Terrace?"

The chief confirmed that Reeve was an orderly there. "I don't want you talking to him—on the phone or in person," he warned. "I'm taking over the investigation here. Are we clear on this?"

Reluctantly I said yes. Then I told Bess what Chief McGinnis had said. Bess glanced over at Davy's little yellow car. "I know there's nothing you'd rather do than charge up to that front door and bust Davy Reeve," she told me. "But you can't. He's a criminal, Nancy. And your dad would never forgive me if I let you get hurt. Besides, look at the time." She showed me her watch. "You'll be late for dinner—again. And so will I if you don't get me home a.s.a.p."

I sighed. Bess was right. Suddenly a thought occurred to me. "I'll be right back," I said. Opening my car door, I dashed across the street to Davy Reeve's vehicle. I peered into the window on the driver's side. Sure enough, the front seat was littered with junk, including several packs of strawberry flavored bubble gum.

"Davy Reeve must be the Cardinal Corners intruder," I told Bess as I got back into my car.

"But is he working alone or with someone else, like Doug Spradling, for instance?" she asked.

We discussed the case until I pulled into the Marvins' driveway. As Bess got out of the car and waved good-bye, another sudden thought came to me. I called directory assistance on my cell and asked for the number of the Fern Terrace Nursing Home. I was punching in the number when Bess turned around and came over to my side of the car. She was scowling as she tapped on the window.

"What are you doing?" she asked suspiciously.

"I'm calling the nursing home," I told her.

"Nancy, you promised!" she said.

"I promised not to talk to Davy Reeve," I reminded her. "But the chief didn't say I couldn't talk *about* him. I'm calling his boss."

Unfortunately the director of the home had left for the day, as had the personnel coordinator. I was advised to call back in the morning around nine to make an appointment.

"Go home," Bess commanded. "We'll talk tomorrow."

Bess was right. There was nothing more I could do today. Waving good-bye, I backed out of the driveway and drove home. There was a battered pick-up truck parked across from my house. It looked vaguely familiar. Then I noticed Juan Tabo sitting in the driver's seat and realized I'd seen this same truck parked at the Olsens' each time I'd been out there.

Wonder what he wants, I thought. I guess I'll just have to ask. But as I got out of my car, Juan took off with a lurch and disappeared down the street and around the corner.

I stood staring after the truck for a moment before going into the house.

"Did you see that truck parked across the street, Hannah?" I asked after making my way to the kitchen, which was filled with the delicious aroma of lasagna baking. Hannah nodded and then replied, "That old battered thing? It was there for nearly twenty minutes before you arrived. I noticed the lawn mower in the bed of the truck and thought perhaps the driver was coming to mow the lawn for someone on the street. But he sat there so long, I decided he must be waiting for you or your father to come home."

"The driver was Juan Tabo, the Olsens' gardener," I told her. Helping myself to an olive from the antipasto tray, I added, "If he was waiting to speak with me, why did he take off when I got out of the car?"

"Well then, maybe he came to see Mr. Drew," Hannah proposed.

"Hmm, why would Juan Tabo need a lawyer?" I mused aloud.

"Maybe he's stalking you," Hannah proposed nervously. "Maybe he's your mysterious caller."

I shrugged and popped another olive in my mouth. When the phone rang a moment later, I answered it while Hannah put garlic bread in the oven. It was Ms. Waters calling to tell me about her conversation with Luther Eldridge. Chuckling, I told her that Luther had driven out to Cardinal Corners and "delivered" his information personally.

"When I left this afternoon, the Olsens were giving him the grand tour of the old place," I said. Briefly I told her about the discovery of the tunnel and thanked her for her help. Because Hannah was listening, I left out the part about being conked on the head. I didn't want her to worry, and I sure didn't want her to tell my dad about the incident either.

"A secret tunnel!" Hannah exclaimed. "How exciting!"

I repeated the story again for my dad during dinner. Intrigued, he and Hannah listened wordlessly as I told them about the storm cellar in the woods, the crawl space in the Olsens' basement, and the dumb-waiter. My dad raised an eyebrow when I mentioned that we'd caught the gardener eavesdropping too.

"Juan Tabo isn't one of your clients, is he?" I asked, passing him the basket of garlic bread.

"No, he's not," my father replied. "Why do you ask?"

"Hannah told me that he was parked outside for some time," I said. "When I pulled into the driveway, he took off. I wondered if he'd wanted to see you and then decided not to wait."

"If he calls the office tomorrow or drops in, I'll certainly let you know," my dad said. "Do you suspect him of having anything to do with the vandalism? I thought you'd pretty well decided that this fellow Davy Reeve is your intruder."

I nodded. "But there are a few things about Juan that bother me. He hasn't exactly been friendly, and he has reason to be upset with the Olsens—he didn't get the raise he asked for."

114

"And he listens at keyholes," Hannah pointed out, bringing in lime sherbet for dessert.

"Dad, do you think Chief McGinnis will pick up Davy Reeve?" I asked.

"Only for questioning," he replied. "You can't arrest someone just because you think they are guilty. You have to have proof."

"But we don't have any," I said. "Except for the bubble gum wrappers."

"That's called circumstantial evidence," my father reminded me. "They won't arrest Reeve for that."

Immediately after dinner, I called Mrs. Mahoney and told her about the discovery of the tunnel and everything else that had happened that day.

"With the storm cellar padlocked and the dumbwaiter disabled and the new security system installed, I'm sure nothing else will happen between now and Saturday afternoon," she said. "On behalf of the entire committee, I want to express my heartfelt thanks, Nancy."

I murmured an embarrassed "you're welcome" and decided to take a long, hot shower. I washed my hair, too, being very careful not to press too hard on the bump at the back of my head, which was still tender. I kept thinking of what my dad had said about evidence. Even if Chief McGinnis brought Davy Reeve in for questioning, he couldn't arrest Reeve on circumstantial evidence. Reeve would have to confess, and what were the chances of that happening?

I had just wrapped my hair in a towel when the phone rang. I picked up the extension on the night table beside my bed. "Hello?" I said.

"Nancy Drew?" The deep voice belonged to a man.

"Yes, this is Nancy," I replied cautiously. "Who is this?"

"Never mind—this is your second warning to stay way from Cardinal Corners. There won't be another one." The man's voice was unmistakably threatening.

"Is this Davy Reeve?" I asked boldly.

There was complete silence on the other end of the line and then a loud click. My anonymous caller had hung up. Lost in thought, I did the same.

So my hunch was right, I thought, chewing on my bottom lip. The intruder or intruders were determined to get their hands on something inside the Olsens' house. A padlock on the storm cellar doors would not deter them. He—or they—would try again.

But I had an idea. Picking up the phone again, I tapped out a number I knew as well as my own.

"Ned, it's Nancy and I need a favor," I said.

13

Old Wives' Tales

First thing the next morning I called the Olsens. I wanted to make sure there had been no break-in during the night.

"Everything's fine, Nancy," Mrs. Olsen assured me. She sounded quite cheerful. "The padlock on the storm cellar door must have worked."

"I'm not so sure it was the padlock," I told her.

"What do you mean?" she asked.

"I'll explain later," I said.

After breakfast I dressed carefully in my new suede skirt and matching blue blazer and made my way to the Fern Terrace Nursing Home. I had no trouble at all getting a spur-of-the-moment appointment with the director, Mattie Burney. She was a plump, middle-aged woman with a no-nonsense manner.

"What can I do for you?" she asked, removing her glasses. She indicated a chair across from her desk and motioned for me to have a seat.

"My name is Nancy Drew, and I'm looking into vandalism that has occurred at the Cardinal Corners bed-and-breakfast," I told her.

"That's where the fund-raiser is going to be held, isn't it?" she asked. "I have two tickets." Then on a more serious note, she added, "I wasn't aware that the place had been vandalized. I haven't heard or read anything about this in the news."

"The Olsens don't want any unfavorable publicity," I explained.

"I don't see how I can help you," Mrs. Burney said. She relaxed in her leather chair and folded her hands in her lap.

"One of your employees, an orderly named Davy Reeve, is a suspect in the case," I said.

Mrs. Burney raised an eyebrow.

"If you don't mind, I'd like to ask you a few questions about him," I continued.

"But I do mind," she replied curtly, sitting up straighter. "I'm not certain that my board of directors would approve of me speaking to you about any of our employees. Personnel records are private and confidential. When and *if* the police come here with a warrant for Mr. Reeve's arrest, I'll answer their questions at that time—not before."

She pushed her chair away from her desk and stood up. I was clearly being dismissed.

"Thank you for your time," I said, trying to conceal my frustration. A moment later I was standing in the lobby idly watching elderly residents and nurses moving up and down the corridors. What a waste of time! I thought angrily. Now what?

Just then an orderly passed me in the hall. He was pushing an old man in a wheelchair. I suddenly remembered that Doug Spradling, Emily's husband, was an orderly here too. I hadn't promised Chief McGinnis that I wouldn't speak to him, so I asked a passing nurse if he was on duty now and where I could find him.

"Down the hall I think," she told me vaguely before hurrying on.

I hesitantly peered into a number of rooms. Then I saw a large swinging door. When I pushed it slightly open, I could see a tall, broad-shouldered orderly preparing to assist an elderly man into the tub. I quickly stepped back and closed the door. I was not going to interrupt Doug Spradling now. Besides, that single glance at his broad back and beefy arms convinced me that Spradling was much too big to squeeze into the Olsens' dumbwaiter. He couldn't be the Cardinal Corners intruder. Of course he could still be an accomplice, I reasoned.

I had every intention of speaking with him later, but I didn't want to hang out in the corridor. Director Burney would not be pleased if she caught me. With a sigh, I made my way to the visitors' lounge. It was sunny and spacious, with several couches, comfortable chairs, and a big-screen television. Two very old ladies sat hunched at a table playing cards.

As I paused in the doorway, one of them called out, "Are you looking for your granny, sweetheart?"

I smiled and walked over to their table. "Good morning," I said cheerily. "I'm waiting to speak with an orderly."

"Have a seat, honey," one of the women said. "My name is Maude and this is my sister, Thelma." Both had wispy white hair, and their pink sweaters matched.

"My name's Nancy," I told them, walking toward their table. "I'm here to see Doug Spradling." I watched them carefully, looking for some reaction.

"Sure, we know him," Thelma said. "Big fella."

"He could hunt bear with a stick, that one," Maude put in.

"Runs around with that little squirt called Davy," Thelma added. "He has a nasty beard."

When the two old ladies started talking disap-provingly about other staff members with facial hair, I began to wonder how I could gracefully slip away. It was obvious that they weren't going to be much help.

But then Thelma spoke up. "Doug's wife works at the old Rappapport place, doesn't she?"

That caught my attention, and I spoke up quickly, "The bootlegger's house, right?"

Maude and Thelma nodded. I pulled up a chair and sat down. "I've been out there," I said casually. "The new owners are fixing it up. Someone told them that there's probably money hidden in canning jars all over the basement."

"Sure, old man Rappapport didn't trust banks, you know," Thelma said. "He stashed wads of money in every nook and cranny."

"Our daddy used to buy hooch from him during the Prohibition years," Maude explained. She chuckled reminiscently. "Bathtub gin," she added with a smirk.

"I heard that the police confiscated all the money when they arrested Mr. Rappapport for bootlegging," I said.

Maude cackled. "Don't count on it—Leon was a clever old fox. Our father said so."

"Don't put all your eggs in one basket," Thelma added with a knowing wink.

121

"People snooped around that place for years looking for Rappapport's secret stash," Maude said.

"Did they ever find anything?" I probed.

The two old ladies laughed again. "They wouldn't tell if they did," Thelma said.

When I pressed for more details, they didn't have any to offer. Could there really be money still hidden in the old house somewhere? If Mr. Rappapport had a secret tunnel, could he have had a secret hiding place, too?

While the two sisters shuffled their cards and talked about Prohibition days, I began to wonder about loose bricks around the fireplace and other possible places where one could hide a wad of cash. I was gazing absently out the window when I noticed Doug Spradling outside underneath the portico. He was pushing an elderly man in a wheelchair. I quickly excused myself and dashed outside to speak to him.

But he definitely didn't want to speak with me. I walked up to him and said, "Mr. Spradling, my name is Nancy Drew." He turned as white as his uniform and took a step backward. "I'd like to ask you a few questions," I said.

"I'm not supposed to talk to you," he replied gruffly. "I'll get into trouble."

"Who told you not to talk to me?" I asked.

"Can't tell," he said.

"I think you've been calling my house and making threats," I said on a whim.

Spradling's eyes bulged from their sockets. He looked afraid. "If you don't leave me alone, I'll tell my boss that you're harassing me," he said nervously.

He hurried away, pushing the wheelchair briskly. Once, he glanced over his shoulder at me. I didn't follow him. If he went to the director and told her I was bothering him, things could get very unpleasant.

However, the morning had not been a complete loss, I told myself as I drove to George's house. Maude and Thelma had been pretty informative, in a chatty sort of way. Listening to them had given me an idea. I had a hunch that the intruder would try again if he was convinced that there was still money inside the house. And he would try again before Saturday because by then the empty bedrooms at Cardinal Corners would be filled with paying guests, and hunting for the bootlegger's hidden stash would definitely become more difficult.

I called Mrs. Olsen on my cell and told her about my idea. "If my hunch is correct, the intruder will be desperate to search your house before all the guests start arriving on Saturday," I said. "He didn't come last night—so that gives him tonight and tomorrow night. I want to catch him in the act."

Mrs. Olsen readily agreed to let George, Bess, and

me sleep at the house that night and the next in an effort to catch the intruder. "I've got fresh sheets on all the beds," she said. "Bring your pajamas."

While I was on my way to George's house, Ned called. "Hey, Nancy, when can I get my car back? And did it work—my leaving it out there on the road by the river?"

I grinned. "Yes, it worked. There were no ghostly pranks pulled at Cardinal Corners last night. You can pick up your car anytime—the sooner the better." I briefly explained my plan for the evening and thanked him for his help.

"Be careful," he warned. I could hear the concern in his voice.

I promised I'd be extra careful. Before saying good-bye, I asked, "Aren't you going to give me one tiny hint about Saturday's surprise?"

I heard Ned's throaty chuckle and could easily envision his adorable dimples. They're very noticeable when he laughs. "No clues, Nancy. You'll have to wait until Saturday," he said.

When I arrived at George's house, I found her taking inventory of the dozens of teacups, saucers, and matching dessert plates her mother intended to use for Saturday's tea. One of Mrs. Fayne's employees was filling plastic bins with home-baked scones.

"You remember Susan, don't you, Nancy?" George asked.

I nodded and said hello to the young woman with the long dark ponytail. "The scones smell delicious," I said. When Susan asked if I'd like to sample one, I eagerly accepted.

"This is the best scone I've ever tasted," I declared. "It's so moist. What's your secret?"

"We use yogurt in the dough," Susan said with a smile. Then she turned away to check on another batch in the oven.

I waited until she was out of earshot before speaking quietly to George. "We're going back out to Cardinal Corners tonight—I've arranged it all with Mrs. Olsen," I told her. "We'll remove the padlock and have Bess fix the dumbwaiter. Then we'll catch Davy Reeve in the act of breaking in. The police will have to arrest him then."

"Nancy, I can't," George said with a slight wail. "There's too much left to do, and I promised my mom I'd help. There's still silverware to polish and sugar cubes to decorate and lots of other things. Call Bess."

I did. Bess was available and more than willing for another adventure. "I'll pack an overnight bag, and you can pick me up after dinner," she said.

On my way home I stopped by my dad's office and told him what I planned to do that evening. He was on his way to meet a client for lunch, so I didn't keep him long. "Catching him in the act is the only way I'm going to convince the police that Davy Reeve is the Cardinal Corners vandal," I said. "And I'm pretty sure Doug Spradling is in on it too. He wasn't at all happy to see me at Fern Terrace this morning."

"Davy Reeve has a criminal record. He could be dangerous, Nancy," he said with a frown. "You'll have to be on your guard."

"I'll stay alert," I promised.

I didn't think to call Luther Eldridge again until I was packing my overnight bag. When I told him what Maude and Thelma had said, he agreed that Leon Rappapport had probably stashed money all over the house.

"Any suggestions where I should look?" I asked.

"Hmmm, that's hard to say," Luther said. "Check for wobbly bricks around the fireplaces and loose floorboards, I guess."

I thanked him and hung up. Mrs. Olsen called as I was rummaging around in the refrigerator for a snack. "Why don't you girls come for dinner tonight," she said. "I make a mean meatloaf."

I started to tell her that it would only be Bess and me when I had a sudden brainstorm. "George isn't able to come, but would you mind if I invite Luther Eldridge?" I asked.

"Good idea, Nancy," Mrs. Olsen said. "The more the merrier."

When I called him back, Luther was thrilled. "Nancy, I feel like an amateur sleuth," he joked. He assured me that he'd meet me at Cardinal Corners promptly at six.

"Bring a flashlight and extra batteries," I reminded him before saying good-bye.

I retrieved my own flashlight—one nearly as long as my arm—and an extra set of batteries. But I had no intention of packing pajamas, as Mrs. Olsen had suggested. To be honest, I didn't expect to get much sleep that night. Instead I changed into sweats with a matching cami and my favorite sneakers. Tonight was the night! I just knew it. The "ghost" of Cardinal Corners was going to be vanquished once and for all!

14

Tense Moments

Dinner at the Olsens' that evening was rather festive. Luther and Mr. Olsen had removed the padlock from the storm cellar, and Ned had come for his car. Bess had reconnected the dumbwaiter's pulleys too. But she'd also slipped a wedge between the small elevator and the shaft. When the intruder got in, he wouldn't be going up.

Everyone was in such a good mood that we seemed to forget the possible dangers ahead of us. Things could get ugly. I'd already been conked on the head once. I didn't want it to happen again. Mr. Olsen must have seen the worry on my face, because while we were having peach cobbler and ice cream for dessert, he said, "Nancy, you seem uneasy. What's the matter?"

"We shouldn't be overconfident," I replied. "We haven't caught the prowler yet. Reeve may come armed with a knife or gun. We need to be careful."

With this sobering thought, we discussed our plans for the long night ahead. Afterward Mrs. Olsen showed us to our rooms on the second floor. Bess and I shared one with two twin beds. Luther had the room next to ours.

"This is a beautiful armoire," Bess said, hanging her clothes inside the huge oak wardrobe. It had panels of art deco stained glass on the front. "It must be a real antique!"

Remembering what Luther had said about the bootlegger's money still being hidden in the house somewhere, I asked Mrs. Olsen about the armoire. "Did it come with the place?"

"Yes, it did. Apparently it was too heavy to move," she said. "Despite the nicks and scratches, it's a lovely old piece. One of these days Karl is going to refinish it."

I inspected the wardrobe carefully, knocking on all the panels and opening the drawers.

"Hmmm, this drawer looks a bit shallow, doesn't it?" I asked.

"Shallow?" Mrs. Olsen said. "What do you mean?"

"Bess, hand me your nail file," I said.

"Just don't break it," Bess said, giving me the file. I tried sliding it along the bottom edge of the drawer to see if I could pry the drawer up. It wouldn't budge.

"Nancy! Don't bend my nail file," Bess squealed. I sighed. There was no time to fool around with the drawer anyway. I had plans to finalize and an intruder to catch. At around ten o'clock, we all retired to our own rooms and turned off the lights. If anyone was watching the house from the woods, he would think we'd all gone to bed.

I retrieved my long, heavy-duty flashlight from my overnight bag. "Sure hope this works," Bess whispered as she grabbed the sleeping bags and followed me down the stairs in the dark.

"Me too," I said.

"What if Davy Reeve doesn't show up?" she asked quietly.

"Then we'll have to try again tomorrow night," I whispered back.

Downstairs, we checked on Mrs. Olsen, who was curled up on one end of the sofa in the dark parlor, armed with her flashlight and cell phone. "Ready for action," she said.

As planned, Mr. Olsen and Luther were bunking down in the living room. "I've turned off the security alarm," Mr. Olsen said. "But I don't think he'll come in through the back door. He's going to come in through the tunnel, and you girls will be all alone down there in the basement. I don't like it."

"Me neither," said Luther. "Karl and I should hide in the basement and you girls stand guard in the parlor."

"Do either of you know karate or judo?" Bess asked.

Even in the dark, we could see both men shake their heads. "Do you?" Mr. Olsen asked.

"Bess and I have taken classes," I replied. "So we can handle ourselves. But we're leaving the basement door open, just in case. When you hear us call out, come running."

Bess and I didn't turn on our flashlights until we opened the basement door and started down the steps. We didn't want Davy Reeve—if he was watching—to see the beams of light through the windows and get suspicious. We positioned our sleeping bags in a strategic location against the far wall. We didn't crawl into them, but merely used them as a cushion against the cold hard basement floor. We'd be able to see the intruder as he opened the door to the crawl space, but he wouldn't be able to see us. At least that was the plan.

"Whatever we do, we can't let Davy Reeve escape through the tunnel," I told Bess. "Make sure he's already in the dumbwaiter before we rush him. And one of us should be sure to close the door to the crawl space.

"I'll do that," Bess offered, squirming around for a more comfortable position. "I sure hope he comes. I don't want to spend two nights down here on this hard old floor."

I chuckled. Then, leaning back against the wall, I placed the long flashlight across my lap and said, "He'll come tonight. You'll see."

I had no idea how long I'd been sleeping when the sound of something moving in the crawl space woke me. I went from groggy to alert instantly. With my heart pounding and my pulse racing, I nudged Bess with my elbow. She sat up immediately and clutched my arm. Then she squeezed it. That was her signal that she was ready and waiting. So was I.

Slowly the small door to the crawl space creaked open. A short man wearing all black—including a black ski mask—slipped through the door. He held a flashlight in one hand and a tire iron in the other. I could hear Bess's irregular breathing. She was nervous. So was I. If Davy Reeve decided to look around the basement with his flashlight, he'd see us for sure. I hoped that he would make his way immediately to the dumbwaiter, and he did. When I felt Bess move beside me, I placed a warning hand on her knee. We were not supposed to spring our trap until Reeve opened the door of the dumbwaiter and climbed inside.

Clenching his flashlight now in his teeth, the intruder started to climb into the dumbwaiter. As he was lifting his leg in, I whispered, "Now," and together Bess and I sprung from our hiding place. We flicked on our flashlights and bolted toward him. Bess slammed the door to the crawl space shut as we dashed past.

"Stop where you are!" I cried out. The man stumbled backward and spun around. I turned my flashlight straight in his face. He gave a startled cry and threw up his hands to shield his eyes from the glaring beam. Bess snatched his ski mask off.

"Davy Reeve, I presume?" she quipped. The small man with the heavy red beard glared at us wordlessly.

"Come on out of there," I said. "Bess disabled it. You're not going anywhere."

With a snarl, Davy Reeve lashed out with his own flashlight and nearly hit Bess in the face. She stepped back just in time. Then things began to happen all at once. Bess hollered out for Mr. Olsen just as Reeve lunged at me, his fists flying. I ducked and spun around before grabbing the tire iron out of his hand. Reeve was shorter than me, but quick and wiry. He pushed me so hard that he knocked me off my feet.

"Don't let him get away, Bess!" I shouted as I fell.

Bess tackled him as I scrambled to my feet. Grabbing the nearest thing I could find to tie him up with—which turned out to be a string of Christmas tree lights—I flung myself on top of Reeve as he wriggled savagely. Bess sat down on him as hard as she could and held down his legs. I'd just finished binding Reeve's wrists when Mr. Olsen and Luther came clomping down the basement stairs. They flicked the switch, and in an instant the basement was flooded with light.

"Good work, girls!" Luther and Mr. Olsen declared with admiration.

Davy Reeve turned his head, trying to cover his eyes. The arrival of the two men seemed to take the fight out of him. His shoulders slumped and he quit moving.

"I don't trust him," I said, brushing my hands off. "Wish we had a pair of handcuffs."

"Will duct tape do?" Bess asked. She pulled a roll off one of the shelves, and after a brief scuffle with Reeve, we finally succeeded in binding his ankles.

"Your wife should call the police now," I said, turning to Mr. Olsen.

"The police are already here, Nancy," Mrs. Olsen called out from the top of the stairs. She smiled down at me and stepped aside. To my surprise, Officer Madison was right behind her, along with Juan Tabo and a sulky Doug Spradling. I noticed the handcuffs around Spradling's wrists.

"Wow, that was fast!" I declared, hurrying up the stairs. "Where'd you find him?" I asked, pointing to Spradling.

"He was waiting in a car down by the river," Officer Madison told me.

"A bright yellow car," Juan added with a grin. "I've been hiding down near the river all night. When I saw the same yellow car I told you about earlier, I went out to the road and flagged this officer down as he drove by."

"Mr. Drew called Chief McGinnis this afternoon and suggested the police patrol this area tonight," Officer Madison explained. "I volunteered."

"We sure appreciate your help," I said. Turning to Juan, I added, "And yours, too, Juan. Why did you come to my house yesterday and then drive away before I could speak to you? How'd you know where I live?"

"Your dad's name is in the phone book, and I wanted to volunteer to help you catch that guy," he said, pointing to Davy Reeve, who was sitting on the bottom step. "I do yard work for a family that lives a few streets over from yours, so I decided to stop in and see you while I was in the neighborhood. It dawned on me when I got there that you probably had my name on your list of suspects. That's when I saw you coming down the street. I was embarrassed and so I left," Juan explained.

Leaving me and Juan to keep an eye on Doug Spradling, Officer Madison went downstairs and officially arrested Davy Reeve. Relieved, Bess hurried up the stairs and gave me a hug. Luther and Mr. Olsen came up after her. Then the policeman, with his suspect in custody, came up last of all.

"You weren't a very convincing ghost," Bess said to Reeve as Officer Madison escorted him into the kitchen.

"Emily was convinced," Davy retorted. "She's so scared she's afraid to come back to work. That's what she told her husband."

"No challenge there," I said. "Why all the pranks anyway, and what were you looking for?"

"Money," Reeve replied. He went on to tell us what he'd learned of the bootlegger's stash. He knew nothing we didn't already know. "I wanted to scare the Olsens out of the house. There's still a room upstairs I haven't searched yet."

"All the money was confiscated years ago when the authorities raided the place," Luther told him. "You wasted your time."

"Can't fault a guy for trying," Davy said with a shrug.

"Oh, yeah?" I said. "You have no respect for private property. You broke a lot of teapots that didn't belong to you, and that booby trap on the back staircase could have caused a serious injury."

Davy Reeve said nothing, but he and Doug Spradling exchanged guilty looks.

"Are you the one who conked Nancy on the head?" Bess asked with a frown.

Reeve nodded.

"And the anonymous phone calls to me and the Olsens?" I asked.

Davy Reeve nodded again.

"I still don't understand why you shattered the teapots," Bess said. "In ghost stories, the spooks usually break mirrors."

"I told him not to break any mirrors," Doug Spradling spoke up. "Seven years' bad luck."

I laughed. "You'll get seven years' bad luck all right," I said, nodding to Officer Madison.

15

Tea Is Served

After the police hauled away the Cardinal Corners culprits in a squad car, Mrs. Olsen served us hot chocolate and cookies in the kitchen. We were exhilarated by our success, but tired, too, and we went to bed shortly after stacking our dishes in the sink.

Bess and I slept in until nine o'clock the next morning. Glancing at the time, I immediately called my dad at home to tell him what had happened the night before.

"Another case successfully solved. Good work, Nancy." I could hear the pride in his voice.

"Thanks, Dad," I replied. "And thanks for having Chief McGinnis send the patrol car."

When I got up to get dressed, I glanced down at that last drawer again while retrieving my clothes from the armoire. Too impatient to wait, I ran down to the kitchen and got a butter knife. I went back upstairs and now Bess joined in, helping me wedge the knife into the bottom of the drawer.

Mrs. Olsen came upstairs to tell us she'd made waffles for breakfast. She found Bess and me on the floor, battling with her armoire.

"Girls, be careful. That's a valuable antique," Mrs. Olsen warned.

Once we'd managed to build up enough leverage, the piece of wood popped up with a jerk.

"Oh dear!" Mrs. Olsen exclaimed. "Did you break it?"

"Not quite," I replied, pulling up the wood to reveal the drawer's hidden section.

Her mouth dropped open when I pulled a gray sock out of the back. It was fat and lumpy and obviously stuffed with something.

"What do you think is inside?" I asked, handing it to her.

"I can guess!" Bess declared. "The bootlegger's forgotten stash."

Bess was right. Mr. Olsen counted the wad of bills and smoothed them out at the table while we ate. There was almost two thousand dollars.

"That was a small fortune back in the twenties," Luther said later over coffee.

"I can't believe it, Nancy!" Mr. Olsen declared. "You caught the intruders and discovered old man Rappapport's money, too. We don't know how to thank you."

Lifting his glass of orange juice, he proposed a toast. "Three cheers for Nancy Drew—detective extraordinaire!"

Everyone raised their glasses and cheered. I blushed. I was greatly relieved to have solved the riddle of the broken teapots in time for the fund-raiser to take place as planned. Finding the money in the armoire was just a lucky coincidence.

On our way home, Bess and I stopped by Julia Jute's place to pick up our gowns for the tea. "George will be sorry she missed all the excitement," Bess said when I dropped her off at her house.

"At least she'll be with us when the last mystery in this case is solved," I replied.

Bess frowned and asked, "What are you talking about?"

"Ned's surprise," I said, smiling. I'll admit I was more than a little curious.

At home Hannah was waiting eagerly to hear about my adventures from the night before. She admired my gown for the tea and was particularly relieved when I told her that Juan Tabo had not been stalking me. Mrs. Mahoney was thrilled too with my report and promised to inform the committee that the tea would go on as planned.

"I'm really looking forward to the event," she told me.

"So am I," I admitted.

The next day, I took my time getting ready. I curled my hair and let Hannah help me pin it up. Then she wrapped a ribbon around my head and fastened a cameo necklace around my neck.

"Nancy, you look beautiful!" Hannah declared.

I smiled at my reflection in the mirror. I didn't look like myself at all. I'd been transformed into a character from one of Jane Austen's novels.

Cardinal Corners was transformed too. There were potted flowers and garlands and satiny ribbons on the veranda. Inside, dozens of small tea tables had been set up and draped with chintz table linens. Each was decorated with one of Ms. Waters's floral bouquets. Even the sugar cubes were decorated with candied violets.

George, very stylish in her red spencer, and Bess, beautiful in blue, were already there when I arrived. "You girls look lovely," Mrs. Olsen complimented us. Her husband insisted on taking our picture.

In the kitchen Mrs. Fayne was quietly commanding

her efficient troop of kitchen help. I was astonished to find Emily Spradling in the kitchen too, carefully placing little pink cakes on a doily-covered platter.

"I'm surprised to see her here today," I said softly to Mrs. Olsen.

"The poor thing called yesterday in tears," Mrs. Olsen said. "Emily told me she was horrified by her husband's arrest and totally ignorant of what he and Davy Reeve had been doing. I feel sorry for her, Nancy."

"Do you think you can trust her?" I asked, glancing in Emily's direction.

Mrs. Olsen followed my gaze. "Yes. I'm certain she's guilty of nothing more than stupidity," she said. "The poor woman has left her husband and moved in with her mother. She's even offered to pay for the damaged teapots."

As paying guests started to arrive, Mrs. Mahoney and Ms. Waters, wearing beautiful Regency costumes, greeted them at the door. George, Bess, and I stayed busy taking tea orders and carrying delicious refreshments to each table. Everyone admired our dresses and *oohed* and *aahed* over the food.

"These are beautiful tarts!" Bess declared when Mrs. Fayne gave us platters to carry into the parlor.

"But there's no bullet pudding," George said as she passed by with a plate of scones. Bess and I laughed and pretended to pout.

I was carefully carrying a bunny-shaped teapot to a table of chattering women in the back of the parlor when Bess hurried by and whispered, "Ned's here!" She was grinning from ear to ear.

I set the bunny teapot down carefully on the table and rushed to the front door as fast as my long dress would allow. Ned, his mother, Deirdre, and Mrs. Shannon were standing in the foyer shaking hands with Agnes Mahoney. My mouth dropped open as soon as I saw him. Ned was wearing an authentic Regency period costume, complete with tan-colored pantaloons and knee-high boots. He looked so handsome! All the ladies thought so, and they made quite a fuss over him. Deirdre was clinging to his arm like a barnacle to a ship.

Seeing me, Ned smiled and raised a hand in greeting. He quickly shrugged his arm from Deirdre's grasp and hurried over to me. He was blushing a little. "Nancy, you look great!" He took my hands in his. "My mom insisted that you'd get a kick out of seeing me in this getup." He glanced down at his costume and smiled shyly. "This is the surprise."

"Ned, I love it! You're even more handsome than Mr. Darcy," I declared, naming the dashing hero in *Pride and Prejudice.*

"Well, you're more beautiful than Miss Elizabeth Bennet," Ned replied.

"Why, thank you, kind sir," I replied, smiling up at him.

"I think you look awesome too, Ned," Bess said, hurrying past him with a platter of tiny sandwiches.

"Ditto," George declared. Deirdre came up then, trying to reclaim Ned's arm, and George thrust a tray of teacups and saucers at her. "Time to go to work, DeeDee," she said.

Needless to say, the event was a huge success. The costumes set the right tone, and Mrs. Fayne's refreshments received rave reviews. But Ned's surprise was not the only one I received that afternoon. When Mrs. Mahoney announced the generous amount of funds raised for the library, everyone applauded.

But then she added, "Mr. and Mrs. Olsen would like to donate an additional two thousand dollars in honor of Miss Nancy Drew. Without Nancy's perseverance and clever detecting skills, this event would not have been able to take place."

The applause was deafening. To my embarrassment, Mrs. Mahoney made me step forward and take a little curtsy. I made my escape as quickly as possible and found the Olsens on the veranda, waving to departing guests.

"Nancy, we're so pleased with what you've done,"

Mrs. Olsen said, giving me a hug. "We were going to offer you the money found in the armoire as a reward, but Bess and George said you'd prefer that we donate it to the library fund."

"They're right, as usual," I said with a pleased grin.

"We asked Chief McGinnis about it," Mr. Olsen added. "He said they didn't need the money for evidence. The bootlegger's case was solved years ago, and we could do whatever we wanted to with the cash."

I thanked them for their generosity and hurried to the kitchen to find Bess and George.

Later I had a quiet moment alone with Ned. We sat together on the porch swing, drinking tea and sharing a buttered scone.

"All's well that ends well," I said with a happy sigh.

"That's Shakespeare, not Jane Austen," he quipped.

I punched him lightly. "You know what I mean," I said.

"Yes, it's your way of saying, 'Another case solved,'" he replied, putting an arm around my shoulders.

We sat in comfortable silence, listening to the birds chirp and twitter. It had been a wonderful day, and I had enjoyed every bit of it, particularly when Mrs. Shannon left early with one of her friends and insisted on taking Deirdre with them. I hoped the Olsens would live happily ever after at Cardinal Corners. I could relax now too for a while—until the next perplexing mystery came along.

This Fall, take the mystery with you on your Nintendo DS™ system!

NANCY DREW™

The Deadly Secret of Olde World Park

- Play as Nancy Drew, the world's most recognizable teen sleuth
- Solve puzzles and discover clues left by a slew of suspicious characters
- Use the Touch Screen to play detective mini-games and access tasks, maps and inventory
- Unravel 15 intriguing chapters filled with challenging missions and interrogations

THE HARDY BOYS

BOYS

UNDERCOVER BROTHERS™

They've got motorcycles,
their cases are ripped from the headlines,
and they work for ATAC:
American Teens Against Crime.

CRIMINALS, BEWARE:
THE HARDY BOYS ARE ON YOUR TRAIL!

Frank and Joe are telling all-new stories of crime,

danger, death-defying stunts, mystery, and teamwork.

Ready? Set? Fire it up!